Hidden
Truths

Hidden Truths

Jeff Boyle

"To suppress a truth is to give it force
beyond all endurance."

— Chinese proverb

boldventurepress.com

Hidden Truths
This edition published
September 2016

The stories in this collection are
Copyright © 2016 Jeff Boyle. All rights reserved.

Cover design: Rich Harvey

Cover photo by Matee Nuserm
Copyright: Matee Nuserm / 123RF Stock Photo

Illustrations by larysaray
Copyright: larysaray / 123RF Stock Photo

ISBN-13: 978-1537556703
Retail cover price $12.95
Available in eBook edition

Printed and bound in the United States.

Contents

INTRODUCTION

A yearning for connection binds many of the stories in Jeff Boyle's fine collection. His lean, muscular prose reads as smooth as a flat sea. Yet still waters can disguise powerful undertows, and to slip into Boyle's world is to risk being swept away. Let yourself go, and when the current releases you back on shore you'll have more to contemplate than the view of the ocean many of his characters enjoy.

Seeking a common theme in a collection of short stories can be a fool's errand. The editor risks interposing personal interpretations that may obscure the writer's intent or, worse, bias readers in a direction that prevents them from making their own discoveries in the flow of language.

So let's set aside questions of theme. Discover those for yourself. It's in the premise that we find commonalities among Boyle's sixteen stories. In a world where people find themselves increasingly isolated from neighbors and their communities, Boyle shows us again and again characters swimming against that tide to reach some kind of bond with another.

Two retirees who navigate the unfamiliar customs of Internet dating. Young lovers who find insight into their relationship through a shared viewing of a classic film. A man drawn to a bedraggled street evangelist. The elderly patients of an assisted-living facility who bond over Scrabble. A childless couple who contemplate adopting a boy to fill an unstated void. A professor who bonds with his students over a Socratic exchange about the causes of crime. A man and woman whose May-December romance threatens to come crashing down on a discount-airlines flight. Young mall workers who learn about trust and love at the food court.

The stories are told with humor, compassion and an eye for detail that vivify the varied settings. You don't have to take daily bicycle rides on a breeze-cooled beach — as Boyle does — to feel the sun on your shoulders and smell the tang of salt on the air.

Yet it's the characters who linger afterwards. Some find resolution; others don't. Some come away wiser for their experiences; others resist. The struggle animates them. They seek to break down barriers that would seal them into heart-rending loneliness, and in reading their stories, you set them free.

— Derek Catron

*Derek Catron is the author of **Trail Angel**, a historic novel of love and redemption. The novel was published in August 2016 by Five Star Publishing, which will release a sequel in 2017. Read about both books at derekcatron.com.*

This collection is dedicated to

COLLEEN GARRETT

Friend, mentor, writing partner,
author of the novel *Josephine's Garden*

Between the absolute and eternal truths of life and death, we spend our lives seeking, hiding, and revealing smaller truths.

These stories are about such human endeavors.

Jeff Boyle, June 2016
Ormond Beach, Florida

Miss Piano

An endless silent movie passed below as Melissa watched from the fourth floor window of her midtown Manhattan apartment, sipping tea in morning ritual on her fortieth birthday. Warm May sunlight bathed her rooms but had not yet reached the shadowed intersection of Ninth Avenue and Fifty-fifth, where oblivious pedestrians herded through breaks in heavy Friday traffic pouring from the Upper West Side.

Morning solitude sealed off the city's urgent pace and allowed quiet dismissal of an upcoming, insignificant Mothers' Day. Childless and an only child, Melissa had no family, special friend, or lover to celebrate birthday or holiday. Her father had disappeared before she was born and her mother died in a swimming pool, drowned by alcohol, pills, and despair.

Instead, Melissa celebrated the grandmother who raised her, remembering sun drenched mornings in her mansion on Long Island. Geema knitted and patiently answered her grandchild's questions about missing parents and the dead grandfather never met. She was told her mother had been away on a "journey" in California. One morning news came of her death.

"God had an opening for an angel and needed your mother right away," Geema explained. "She's with your grandfather."

"Is my Daddy in heaven, too?"

The five year-old could be told partial truths. "He might be. We don't know where he is."

"Will we ever find out?"

"Someday, maybe we will."

Melissa was in her teens when she learned the complete truth. No one ever knew her father's identity, not even the mother who abandoned her for a "journey" pursuing drugs and the wrong men. That life lesson became a legacy for the forty year-old daughter who now believed she'd over-compensated with years of love-hating men, never committing to a relationship.

The sun's climb got her moving, leaving further self-examination for the late morning walk. With dark hair tied back and makeup dabbed beneath green eyes, Melissa changed into a warm-up suit that concealed her wallet and keys in zippered pockets. Athletic shoes laced, she grabbed her sunglasses and rejected the elevator for the stairs, exiting the first floor to a symphony of street noise and cooking scents from a nearby Thai restaurant.

She walked north on Ninth Avenue toward Broadway, upstream against waves of southbound taxis, feeling strong enough to hike all the way to Boston. The sound and motion of the city absorbed the rhythm of her steps and invited deeper introspection, calculating benefits of freedom against costs of loneliness. Money and a rewarding career had not diminished a growing sense that something was missing.

Empty sidewalk tables beckoned from an upscale restaurant on Broadway. The first lunch customer, Melissa seated herself. Long walks and a limit of two meals per day maintained her youthful figure, and she placed a guilt-free order for a Monte Cristo sandwich as she handed the pricey menu back to the waiter. She felt no discomfort sitting at a table for one. Half the people in Manhattan lived alone and preferred it that way.

Melissa took her time eating as breezes carried first breaths of summer. She watched passersby and people buying tickets at the nearby Lincoln Center, where she often sat listening to the pianists, eyes closed, mentally watching hands and fingers reach for keys. The concerts were empowering. The piano was her life.

It began on a childhood morning in Geema's sun room, dark clouds rolling in off the ocean. Angry skies rationed faint gray light as thunder kept interrupting their conversation. Melissa ran over to the baby grand piano and plunked a noisy refrain to the rumbles outside, trying to make them go away. Geema slipped behind and caressed the keys into melody, creating a duet.

"You're welcome to play any time, Melissa, but I insist you sit in the proper position at middle C, with correct posture. And you must play with both hands."

"Could I learn to play like you, Geema?"

"Yes, but it will take years of hard work."

Lightening flashed, but it could have been Melissa's light of discovery, a world opened by a grandmother careful not to push or discourage. The child's enthusiasm and aptitude led to the hiring of a local instructor and the rapid progress of a prodigy. Each learned skill increased Melissa's hunger for higher proficiency, despite Geema's cautions to take it slow, to not allow the piano to displace other activities or time for a boyfriend.

The keyboard compensated, a faithful partner through adolescent recitals, high school solos, and admission to a prestigious college for aspiring musicians.

Classical training led to work with orchestras and touring companies, Broadway musicals, and a brief run as an accompanist for a legendary crooner. Since her mid-thirties, Melissa had played jazz, music that loved her back in the delicious freedom of improvisation.

She paid her bill, walked south to Columbus Circle, took a detour through the green space of Central Park. Leafy trees and the scent of freshly mowed grass confirmed the change of season. On Fifth Avenue, she pondered her double life, Melissa with an alias, the stage name "Missy" first given by Geema while scolding a little girl's tantrum. The two names separated public identity from private. No one ever called her by her real name.

She walked eight blocks south, crossed Fifth Avenue, and entered St. Patrick's Cathedral. Tourists on foot outnumbered worshipers in the pews. She lit a candle not for her mother but for Geema, whispering thanks for a spiritual presence on her birthday and all the other days.

Melissa felt her grandmother's approval, even though she would have encouraged marriage and children. There had been men, serial dating with a corporate executive, an airline pilot, a waiter. But she still could not imagine living with anyone. Geema had lived the last half of her own life without husband or child and would surely understand the need to live alone.

She left the Cathedral and took a card from her wallet to check the address of a law office in a nearby building where, in five days, she had an appointment to draw up her will. Even after purchasing the apartment, the substantial inheritance from her grandmother remained intact. Everything would be left to Geema's beloved homeless shelters and charities.

Near Rockefeller Center, lunchtime crowds filled the sidewalks as gridlocked taxis and delivery trucks honked impatiently. Men left jackets in offices and took to the streets in shirtsleeves while women window shopped displays of new summer clothing. Moving with athletic grace, Melissa caught glimpses of her image reflected in storefronts, the warm-up suit drawing appreciative male glances. Men still looked. Age forty had not changed that.

Tourists snapped pictures and throngs of people lined up at a Times Square box office to buy discount tickets to Broadway shows. Her route passed the theater on West 52nd Street where she'd spent months playing in a musical. Good pay but boring work, the situation made worse by her affair with the conductor, a conflicted type finalizing a divorce. The attraction could have been his position of power, her vulnerability, or both. Late for the show's closing party, he'd called to say he wasn't coming, deciding instead to drive home to Connecticut and reconciliation with his wife. Melissa took the call on a dark high rise balcony, his surreal cell phone voice amplified above a canyon of lighted buildings. She had felt relief, not rejection.

Nearing home, she entered a small grocery on Eighth Avenue. Buying a few items at a time avoided heavy bags and the need for lists. Carrying bread, jam, and toothpaste, she climbed her building's stairs to an apartment subdued by afternoon light. A shower and a disc of soft music facilitated a nap, light sleep resisting a chorus of groaning building pipes and muffled street sounds. She woke to arrange her hair, apply cosmetic touches and dress for the evening. She searched the mirror for forty's aging but saw a face with few lines, perhaps preserved by infrequent smiles. A dozen or so visible strands of silver hair promised more in the future.

Melissa selected a black cocktail dress with spaghetti straps and a pearl necklace with matching earrings. The dress was the one she was wearing at the last concert accompanying the crooner, the best paying job she'd ever had. They were in Atlanta, reprising Sinatra's "It Was a Very Good Year." Serenading words about a former lover's perfumed hair that came undone, the singer wandered over to her piano, unpinned Melissa's hair, and pulled down a spaghetti strap. She finished the show before storming the crooner's dressing room.

"Get yourself another girl, Bobby. I'm quitting, effective immediately."

"Is there a problem?"

"I'm a musician, not a stage prop. You made them think we're fucking."

"Aren't you overreacting?"

"No. Have your manager send the check to my New York address."

Geema would have liked a decision about self-respect. Melissa never spent another night on the road, happy to be done with hotel rooms and their lack of cleanliness. Maybe her reaction had been too strong. Men were such a mystery. The missed experience with high school boys might have been a critical learning curve after all.

The dress still fit. She left a light on and took a handbag large enough for her performance shoes, sunglasses, and keys. A black wool cardigan, needed for the cool walk home, made the dress look less conspicuous. She rode the elevator to the street.

Melissa liked taking the long way to work, east to Broadway and south to Times Square, picking her way through five o'clock swarms of people, sometimes tossing a dollar or two in the instrument cases of street musicians. At Forty-Ninth, she walked west and re-crossed Eighth Avenue to a supper club in the middle of the block. A wooden tent sign displayed three photographs, captioned by name and instrument: "Missy Moore, Piano," "Dom Celli, Drums," and "Phil Gordon, Saxophone." Below the pictured musicians, the sign announced "Jazz Nightly Wednesday thru Saturday." A glass case attached to the brick wall beside the entrance posted the dinner menu. High above, a red neon sign guided patrons to "The Jazz Cellar."

She descended the steps and entered a large room with fifty

tables for dining. Two dozen wine barrels functioned as drink tables with elevated chairs. A long bar and small stage lined the far wall. The place was owned by Sweeney, an iconic character whose decor created timeless atmosphere with a brick interior, exposed ceiling pipes, and dark polished wood. Framed, autographed portraits of celebrities hung everywhere. A sound system piped soft recorded jazz.

Melissa sat down at the bar, carefully folded her sweater, changed shoes, and put the items in the bag with her sunglasses. Paid extra to come in early and play for the dinner crowd, her meals were on the house. She ordered grilled salmon, salad, and a slice of cake, the dessert causing Sweeney to scold her like a worried father.

"My Missy is breaking training?"

"Cake is something I do only once a year."

He quickly guessed. "Should I go find a candle?"

"Please don't. You're the only one who knows."

Sweeney beamed. "My piano girl is twenty-nine!"

"If I am, this cellar is the fountain of youth."

Melissa had worked for Sweeney for two years. He grossed enough to pay three nighttime musicians. Engagement lengths varied, jazz players came and went. The good ones moved on to better gigs and those with less talent were replaced. Others just didn't fit, the narcissistic trumpet player, the depressed bass player, the bipolar guitarist who amped too many solos.

The current group meshed well. In five months, Dom Celli had proven himself a skilled and versatile drummer, as adept with cymbals and brushes as he was with the skins. An expressionless heavy smoker, he stepped out to the alley at every break. Sweeney said Dom's day job was over in Jersey, in a deli-sandwich shop he co-owned with a brother.

Saxophonist Phil Gordon had been with them only two months,

and Melissa knew little about him. A substitute teacher, quiet and reserved, Phil kept his thoughts to himself behind an impassive face that looked both familiar and unfamiliar. Talent too big for the room, he was the one most likely to be offered a better job. The guy had been around, but where? Audiences liked his classy manner announcing the music, and he generously shared the solos. Melissa admired his musicianship, a combination of strength and sensitive interpretation.

She finished her meal, went to the piano and lifted the lid as Sweeney switched off the recorded stuff. More than half the dinner tables occupied, she began a medley of old standards, improvising bridges from one to another. Melissa liked to entertain herself, playing melodies to describe the people she saw dining, her keys creating bright sunlight or drops of rain.

Her piano told their stories, two young men debating a decision to come out, a man and a woman ending an affair, a couple thinking about starting one. Anniversaries were celebrated, business deals closed. The goateed man who dined alone every night was the second most interesting man in the world, an aging novelist infatuated with the piano player. Her intuitive touch found something for each person, themes for love won, love lost, or love unrequited.

When Melissa returned to the bar, Sweeney looked pleased. Her playing, undistracted by the clatter of dishes and payment transactions, complemented the meals. Tables emptied and filled again as the cocktail crowd drifted in.

Dom, in white shirt and vest, arrived first, humming a beat as he removed his drum covers and arranged sticks and brushes. Phil, in a dark, open-collared shirt and cream jacket, retrieved his tenor and alto cases from behind the bar and checked his reeds.

Melissa huddled with them briefly as they scripted a loose, unrehearsed plan for the evening. Each would take turns leading the other two, music blending action and reaction.

At nine o'clock, Dom and Melissa took their seats and Phil, holding the tenor sax, cupped the microphone and addressed the audience.

"Welcome to 'The Jazz Cellar.' I'm Phil Gordon, joined by Missy Moore and Dom Celli. Our group has no name and we don't sing vocals. All of us walked in off the street, just like you. We love jamming and making it up as we go along and hope you'll like our sound."

They played soft west coast jazz from another era, exquisite combinations people had come to hear. Their deft interplay created a growing buzz in the room, unabated after short breaks at ten and eleven.

Just before midnight, Phil picked up the alto sax and announced the last number.

"Thanks for making this a great evening. We love your vibe. We're gonna close it out with Dave Brubeck's 'Take Five,' taking you on a five minute trip from yesterday to tomorrow."

Melissa's part repeated intricate chords played in compound 5/4 time, a constant backbeat for the entire piece. A realization hit as she began playing. This time, the story an instrumental tale of a love triangle, was about her:

… *Drum's ride-cymbal and Miss Piano's repetition preceded Saxophone's resonant entry. Conflict developed when Drum and Saxophone each sought to win Miss Piano. She'd suffered so long with no suitors and now there were two. Chords unrelenting, she made no response to either. Introverted Drum, no match for Saxophone's charisma, patiently tried to outlast his rival, promising Miss Piano loyalty and security against Saxophone's seduction. Perceiving her unwavering signature as rejection, Saxophone departed with no note of farewell. With a clear field, Drum's passionate and persistent beats inspired louder volume from Miss*

Piano, nearly breaking her continuity. But then Saxophone returned, his smooth, unexpected reentry stretching lazy, sensual notes, offering to share, not possess Miss Piano. Drum refused to accept the proposed arrangement and abandoned his pursuit. In so doing, he chose for her. Saxophone had been the one for Miss Piano all along...

The three jazz musicians faded the end of "Take Five" and acknowledged a loud ovation, many patrons standing to applaud. The session was over, and so was Melissa's birthday.

Dom and Phil secured their instruments and vanished into the night. Melissa washed up, closed and covered the piano, and changed to her walking shoes. She said goodnight to Sweeney, put on the sweater, shouldered the bag, and climbed the steps to the sidewalk.

Phil was there, waiting.

"I wanted to tell you how great you played, Melissa. I liked your nuance with the Brubeck."

He had somehow learned her given name, possibly from Sweeney.

"Thank you. We were all good, Phil, one of those nights in the zone."

"Guess that's why everything worked so well." He looked down the street for a long moment, then nervously back at her, disguising a question as a statement. "I didn't know if you wanted to go somewhere for a drink, maybe swap life stories."

His shrugged invitation and the safe tone of indifference in his words let her know her decision would be okay either way. But his pleading eyes said otherwise. She could see her answer mattered to him. It mattered very much.

Melissa smiled.

"Yes," she said. "I'd like that."

TWENTY-TWO

The news said twenty-two veterans commit suicide each day, one self-inflicted casualty every sixty-five minutes. This could be the day to join them. Take back control, man up, solve every problem. End the flashbacks, the nightmares, the failures. Write love note apology to wife. Tell her she's better off. Leave the dress uniform on the bed. Get out the piece and load it. Bring a lawn chair to the back yard. Place gun in mouth, pull trigger, all the pain will be gone in a split-second.

They'll hand her a flag as her honorable husband is laid to rest, then process the survivor's benefits. No more waiting months for delayed disability claims. No more drinking the nights away and sleeping it off during the day when she's at work. No more avoiding her company and her hopes for a baby, this woman who still thinks the man who came home from the war is the same one who left, not the stranger who rarely sleeps in her bed now.

She's stopped asking, instead dropping hints about her husband finding a job. No one would hire a guy running mental videos of dead Afghan kids and buddies blown to pieces, scenes they never talked about in training. Improvised explosions set off by an invisible enemy. Bad intelligence and not-so-smart bombs killing the wrong people. Discovering senseless death in heat, cold, fire, ice, lives ended or spared by chance. Videos that won't erase, looping replays of indelible horrors no eyes should ever see, no wife should ever know.

She says, "Talk to a counselor."

Her daily reminder sits by the phone in the kitchen, a symbolic quarter placed beside a card with the phone number for the veterans' crisis hotline. Make the call she says, failing to understand.

Only the weak ask for help.

The strong survive until their will is gone, battles won but souls lost. Nothing left but exhaustion, booze, and disconnected thoughts in a brain so mushed it can't return to active duty, immune to all prescriptions and those sleeping pills they gave out in the combat zone. Warriors deserve the ultimate sacrifice. A bullet allows no do-overs, no chance to reconsider. Mission accomplished, honor restored.

Her twenty-five cent piece on the counter begs otherwise, a plea for a miracle.

Washington's etched profile on the quarter frowns disapproval, a commander who cannot and will not lie. He knows some decisions offer choices so equal the decision comes down to a coin toss. Trust fate and go with it. Let George decide, heads for life, tails for death.

Flip the coin high, watch it bounce and come to rest beneath the table. Retrieve it, hoping to find George face down.

See him smile back with his order, a command to live, give life another chance, start over.

Put down the gun and pick up the phone.

LIFE
EXPECTANCIES

Deteriorating health forced Ben Martin into an assisted living facility. Alone, divorced and retired, struggling to take care of himself, he had no other option. After finding Autumn House, he soon learned its residents viewed the institution more as a place for assisted dying. The name suggested inhabitants humming Sinatra songs, secure and content in their autumn years. Instead, most were deep in the winter of their lives, counting final days at a last known address, aging orphans waiting for death's adoption.

Each departure opened space for a new tenant from a waiting list. Ben's worn-out heart required professional surveillance, daily medications, and constant monitoring. Worried he'd outlive his money, he sold his house and most of his worldly possessions, accumulating enough cash to cover high-cost care over a now shortened life expectancy. He wrote a check to begin his residency and they let him move in as soon as it cleared.

Health problems had exiled Ben to Autumn House after years of life in the fast lane. A high-stress career, two childless marriages, and toxic addictions to beef, booze, and cigarettes had taken a toll. He'd already died on two occasions, brought back to life each time by machines and miracles of modern science.

The Grim Reaper granted him an indefinite continuance for an unknown number of repetitive, sedentary days.

Thankfully, his failing heart left an undiminished brain. Gratitude for a healthy mind was reinforced when he saw patients from the memory wing. They sat in wheelchairs with heads on chests, heavily medicated in semi-conscious states from strokes, dementia, or Alzheimer's. Others never left their rooms, needing assistance to eat, bathe, and perform simple human functions. Ben promised himself he would not let physical problems or despair darken what was left of his borrowed time. Too many people had it worse.

He could still shower, shave, and shuffle off to breakfast every morning under his own power, low on energy but not without hope for a better day. Self-incarcerated, Ben felt lucky to be confined in Autumn House, with its decent food, every conceivable amenity, and an army of nurses and caregivers who kept the near-dead separated from the general population. Unpleasant scents permeated the common areas, but mitigating air fresheners made odors less noticeable over time.

Outside, manicured grounds offered a panorama of green turf and stately trees. In this peaceful setting, he spent mornings sitting in a high-backed wicker chair on the wrap-around porch, studying squirrels and migrating birds, contemplating ironies of human destiny.

Returning to the veranda one morning, Ben discovered Myra Wade, a person he'd never seen before. A newly-arrived care recipient, she sat motionless in a gleaming wheelchair. Beautiful and fragile, the woman had pale skin, translucent hazel eyes, youthful white-blonde hair parted in the middle. Simple earrings, a crisp blouse and a wide-belted skirt complemented her appearance. Drawn to her aura, Ben moved into her line of vision and introduced himself. She rewarded him with a warm, extended smile as she revealed her name and invited him to sit. He moved his chair closer to face her.

"Welcome to Autumn House, Myra. How are you?"

"Alive. I barely survived cancer. They told me there's a chance it might come back. If it does, I need to be where help is near. Why are you here?"

"Two heart attacks, multiple bypasses, blood thinner meds, bad back, weak bladder, you name it. But I can't complain. I'm in recovery."

"Recovery beats the alternative, Ben. As long as we're breathing, we have hope. I see you've retained your sense of humor. That must mean you're winning the battle."

"Barely. The mental adjustments have been difficult. Mornings and nights are okay, but I get depressed in the afternoon. It's such an idle time of day. I feel useless when people out in the real world are working and competing."

"You should take an afternoon nap, like the rest of us," she said.

"It wouldn't help, not in this gloom and doom with so many inmates on death row. Now I've become one of 'em." His voice carried the resigned monotone of a man condemned.

Myra saw it differently. "There's nothing gloomy about brave souls facing death with courage and dignity. They're inspiring."

"I'm thinking it must have taken a lot of inspiration and courage for you to beat cancer. They say the cure is hell."

"It can be. The radiation and chemo cocktails took away my strength. All my hair fell out and grew back frizzy. Now I feel tired every day." She smiled through fatigue.

"You're a survivor, Myra. I'm betting you've had an interesting life."

"It's still interesting. I worked as a university administrator, facilitating and fundraising. My marriage ended in divorce and my husband disappeared. I still don't know if he's alive or dead. My beautiful daughter became a teacher before a drunk driver killed her in California."

"I'm sorry. Losing her must have been devastating."

"I miss her. Her death took away everything. I cried and grieved until I no longer could. Now I find consolation in sweet memories of our time together."

"You never remarried?"

"No. There was Jonathan, an investment banker I met at the end of my career. We were never lovers, but I accompanied him to concerts, galas, and public events. He liked getting into his tux and admiring my gowns. We were constant companions. When I retired, we traveled the world visiting every continent, even Antarctica."

"It's hard to imagine the two of you spending so much time together without ever becoming more than close friends."

"Our friendship seemed perfectly normal, two people bonded by heart and soul. We were in deep spiritual love, sustained by our intellectual attraction."

"You chose friendship over passion."

"Not at first. He never talked about it, but I knew Jonathan saw other women during our early years. Then I met a man with powerful chemistry. We went hot and heavy until I explained why I couldn't date him on Saturday nights. Maybe he believed I would eventually give up Jonathan. That was never going to happen. The arrangement worked until he decided he could no longer share and we parted ways. In the end, forced to make a choice, yes, I rejected passion for friendship."

"No regrets?"

"None."

A tall man in pale green scrubs stepped onto the porch behind the wheelchair and announced, "Dexter here, right on time. Come to taxi you home, Miss Myra."

Wishing to continue their conversation, Ben asked Myra if she might join him for lunch.

"Sorry, I can't. They bring my meals to my rooms. Tomorrow, I've got some routine maintenance scheduled. Why don't we meet back here morning after next? It will be your turn to talk about your life."

"Okay. We have a date."

After she was wheeled her away, Ben sat alone in the dining room reliving their talk, questioning the power of spiritual love and why he'd never experienced it. Eating his turkey sandwich, he could still feel her presence. Reaching for his cherry Jello, he watched it wobble and become still, guessing Myra would look at it and see a metaphor of human resilience, people shaken but somehow able to recover. He wanted to learn from her. Her subtle wisdom promised more surprises.

Ben rejected his regular afternoon moping for the camaraderie of the game room, to see the smiles and hear the laughter as players competed in gin rummy or played blackjack with pennies.

The television on the wall, tuned to CNN, remained muted, leaving the world's problems silent and irrelevant. The card players and knitters seemed immune from troubles and health issues, at least for a few hours.

***

On the second morning, heavy rain fell, enough to make the veranda cold and damp. Ben waited there anyway, until Myra, her smile, and the loyal wheelchair caddy showed up.

"Rain, rain, go away," she said. "Let's stay indoors this morning. I brought a game. We'll find a secluded spot and play Scrabble. You do play Scrabble, don't you Ben?" Her grin and taunting, laughing eyes lured him to a competition.

With Ben following, Dexter navigated Myra to a social area and positioned her chair at a small table, promising to return in an hour. They sat across from each other, Ben assuring Myra he could read the board upside down and insisting she go first. He admired her deft, elegant touch as she removed letters from the bag and meticulously arranged them on her rack, laying down the word *fund* to start the game. Ben pluralized with the word *shin.* Her next three turns produced *fair, shine,* and *pix,* his responses constructed *fairy, tiny,* and *size.* Under their names, he wrote each new total score on a pad which showed him taking an early lead, one hundred points to seventy-three.

"I see you're an experienced player," she said.

"I did crosswords, and we played the game during lulls in contract negotiations."

"That was your profession?"

"Yes. I represented a large supermarket chain, hammering out contracts with unions all over the country. It was a form of high-stakes poker, with agreements reached only at midnight deadlines. Ten more cents an hour for a meat cutters union added up to a million dollars over a contract year. Living a very unhealthy life style, I was arrogant, vain, and easily influenced by peer pressure to be one of the boys. Late hours, alcohol, and reckless infidelities wrecked my marriages."

"You were a company man, giving unconditional loyalty."

"A loyalty unreciprocated after years of saving them millions. A merger with another company eliminated my position, leaving me with a severance package and nothing to do."

Myra earned a triple word score for *bawl,* before playing *fired, aqua,* and *up,* while Ben countered with *wove, cereal, wit,* and *piker.* After eight rounds, he maintained his solid lead, one hundred eighty points to one hundred sixty.

"So Jonathan never made advances but showed you the world. Was he a father figure?"

"He was simply Jonathan, my best friend."

"If you could go back to one destination, which would it be?"

"Machu Picchu. Eight thousand feet up in the Peruvian mountains, Inca ruins from the fifteenth century. I remember the heat from the sun burning my face, despite the cold the winds. I found peace up on the world's roof, a timeless connection with all things eternal."

"I hated travel," he said. "I visited too many cities. The hotel rooms and conference rooms all looked the same. Now I see them again in this nursing home."

They studied the board in silence, reliving past journeys.

"Do you believe in the afterlife?" he asked.

"I feel a spiritual connection to Jonathan and my daughter. I can't say if the source is internal or external. I'm ready for what's next, afterlife or not. What are your beliefs, Ben?"

"I started thinking about God after I nearly died. Now I'm curious, and I've been watching televangelists in the middle of the night, trying to grasp what they're saying."

"Cancer made me prepare. I've already prepaid all my arrangements. They've got my instructions on file down at the office. Jonathan owned a condo on the beach, and I've made provisions for my ashes to be scattered over the ocean there. Have you done anything?"

"No."

"Better get started. I'm surprised they haven't called you in, to get everything down on paper. These people have a business to run. Even death has to be handled efficiently."

Myra made twenty-eight points on her ninth turn, and Ben earned twenty-five. She then played all seven of her tiles at the bottom of the board to earn a fifty point bonus. Building under the last two letters of *cereal,* she used two blanks to spell the word *touting,* for a total score of sixty-three. When her opponent could tally only thirty, Myra had taken the lead for the first time

Ben whistled softly through his teeth as he wrote down the new numbers.

"Unlike you, I can't read upside down," she said. "Tell me the score."

"You're ahead, two fifty-one to two thirty-five. That was one hell of a play."

"I was losing, but I was able to make something out of nothing. Maybe there's some sort of message in that, for both of us."

"You haven't won yet. The game isn't over."

"Yes it is," she said, playing her tiles.

The contest ebbed and flowed over the final six turns, but Myra prevailed, three hundred twenty-eight to three hundred seven, earning his congratulations.

"That was a real shootout, wide open board, neither of us playing much defense, everything going my way until you played that fifty point bonus. I think I've been hustled."

"We had fun, Ben, an hour's distraction from all that dark fatalism you harbor."

"Nothing's changed. For me, my odds are still fifty-fifty, heart attack or stroke. You and I are never walking out of here."

"You're only a prisoner in your own mind. There are so many things you could be doing."

"Care to give me a list?"

"Use the strength you have left to help those who are weaker. Write a book on collective bargaining. Research charities and put them in your will."

They returned the lettered tiles to the bag and packed up the game. Dexter arrived in squeaking sneakers to release the brake on her chair and take her away.

"Myra, you've reinforced my belief about angels. I think they are humans who watch over the rest of us. I like you."

"I like you, too, Ben. I may just be your angel. We should talk about that tomorrow."

He sat at the table long after she left, absorbing her thoughts, thinking about volunteering to read to residents who couldn't, planning strategies to go about writing the book she suggested.

***

The sun returned the next morning but Myra didn't. Ben waited until lunchtime before going to look for her. When he reached the wing where she stayed, he spotted Dexter at the end of the hall, and approached him to ask about his new friend.

"Mr. Martin, I'm sorry to tell you our Miss Myra passed away during the night. She was at peace when I went in to check on her this morning. They've already taken her away."

Overcome with shock, Ben quietly thanked him before sitting down in a nearby chair.

Myra had gone ahead to her pre-planned destiny, dust scattered upon the sea. Maybe their brief time together had brought closure, helping her let go of life. She'd been teaching him, *touting* hope, her decisive Scrabble word no coincidence. Uplifted, he felt inspired to accept her challenge, vowing to live in hope and share it with others. Over a few days he'd met an angel who taught him how to feel love again.

Spiritual love, deep and eternal.

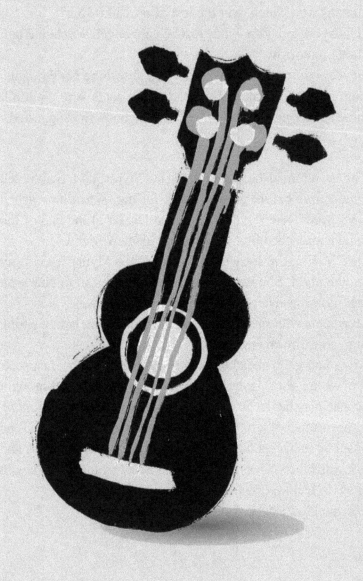

REVERSE
TANGO

February cold gripped Lower Manhattan, steamy vapors rising skyward through the twilight. Standing on a shadowed sidewalk, Mike blew warm breath on his cold hands as he awaited Nikki's arrival from uptown. Their weekend date began every Friday evening in a different location. This week it was Mike's turn to pick the movie and restaurant. Afterwards, they would go to his apartment to spend the night and a lazy Saturday morning in bed, before an afternoon and evening on the town. Nikki would slip out early Sunday morning, and the following week everything would reverse with the sleepover at her place.

Both worked for the same big bank, he at a desk near Wall Street, she as a roving manager troubleshooting branch offices in the Jersey suburbs. They'd met nine months earlier, teaming up at a corporate seminar where employees wore name tags and were taught workplace team building. She liked his humor, he liked her smile.

A cab pulled up and Nikki popped out, clutching a cell phone with the address Mike had texted. The theater behind him, without a marquee or traditional exterior, occupied a small storefront and screened only classic and foreign films. He'd already purchased their tickets, and they kissed and embraced before he escorted her inside. Ignoring the small concession counter, they entered a large room with mostly empty couches and easy chairs, shedding their coats and snuggling into a loveseat, waiting with a handful of other patrons for the show to begin.

"This is cozy. What are we seeing, Mike?"

"Last Tango in Paris, a controversial movie people still talk about."

"When was it released?" she asked.

"Nineteen seventy-two, before we were born. Marlon Brando got a best-actor nomination. The musical score, composed by an obscure Argentine saxophone player who became a jazz legend, backs him with a thirty-six piece orchestra. Fasten your seat belt. I think we'll be seeing some skin."

The theater darkened as a computer projected the film onto a compact screen.

Under misty gray skies, a gray man in a gray coat walks a gray Paris street. He enters a gray building and asks to see an apartment for rent. Taking a key from the concierge, he rides the elevator to an upper floor, where he surprises a young woman already inspecting the flat. They make brief eye contact and tour the rooms separately, slowly circling until their orbits intersect. Here, the film takes a shocking turn when the man, played by Brando, suddenly grabs the woman and passionately pins her against a wall. Two fully-clothed strangers, they kiss and grope their way to upright, writhing sex, the aggressive male reaching for and ripping off the panties of the willing, encouraging female, lifting her, positioning and thrusting. Against the backdrop of a sunless Paris winter, the story alternates scenes of eroticism and despair, punctuated throughout by Gato Barbieri's smoky, sultry saxophone solos. Brando takes the apartment and the woman's carnal offerings in subsequent meetings, their X-rated, full-frontal exercises shattering every previous screen taboo. Inten-

tionally withholding names, the unlikely lovers maintain anonymity as they rendezvous repeatedly to eat, drink, and fornicate. On one occasion, they leave their rented sanctuary and drunkenly crash a ballroom tango contest. In the finale, an obsessed Brando follows the young woman home, breaking the rules of their game by revealing his identity in a declaration of love and possession. Fantasy shattered, fiancé about to return, she thwarts his desperate advance with a gun, mortally wounding her persistent, now threatening lover, watching him death tango to the floor before calmly phoning the police to report an attempted rape.

When the lights came up, Mike helped Nikki with her coat. Exiting the movie house, they bundled up and linked arms, breaths creating small clouds as they clung together tightly for warmth, shielding each other against a brisk north wind on the short walk to an Italian restaurant.

After they were seated, he asked, "Did you like the movie?"

"I should have guessed what I was in for when I saw a make-shift cinema with sofas and stuffed chairs instead of theater seats. I expected something avant-garde but not so graphic. That woman's bush went all the way to her navel."

"Must have been the European style back then," he said. "The nudity and adult content caused problems for the censors. The internet history said they couldn't give the film a rating when it came out but people stood in long lines to see it."

After they ordered a bottle of red wine and their meals, Nikki questioned the movie's plausibility.

"The story was just too surreal," she said. "Two strangers jump each other and have instant sex without even saying 'hello'? It's hard to believe such a spontaneous physical encounter would ever happen in real life."

"Bertolucci claimed it was his personal fantasy. He directed Brando to play a self-absorbed, controlling American, seducing and abusing a sweet French girl. Maybe it was a statement about the sexual revolution going on back then."

"Applause for your sensitive defense of the woman, Mike, but I saw it differently. The guy is shattered by his wife's unexplained suicide, craving any kind of physical intimacy to ease the pain. He's fifty and she's twenty, quite an age disparity. This sexually liberated tart took advantage of a man not in his right mind. Later, finally tiring of the game, she put a bullet through his heart."

"Murder is a common literary theme, always a quick and decisive way to end an affair. Our man never saw it coming. So you're saying he represented good versus her evil."

"She was a player the moment he saw her, flirting and luring with non-verbal signals, letting him know she was willing. When he went for her, she was as hungry for the sex as he was, happy to keep their names secret. But when it's time for her boyfriend to return from an out of town trip, Paul becomes love-crazed and refuses to go away, a huge problem she solves with a gun. Pretty cold-blooded, the way the bitch pulled the trigger and immediately called the police with a ready alibi."

The food came and Mike refilled their glasses, fascinated by Nikki's take on the movie.

"So they're in a virtual reality sex game," he said. "Brando decides he wants more, a commitment, an idea she kills literally as soon as it's suggested, sparing him the emotional pain of rejection. It's ironic the way their relationship ended at the precise moment he asked for it to begin."

"How so?" she asked.

"Doomed relationships usually suffer a long, slow death, beginning with tiny seeds of doubt, discontent growing over time. At some point everything blows up, leaving one or both partners to figure out when or how it all started to go wrong."

Nikki wasn't sure. "I think infidelity, once it's discovered, can kill the chemistry in an instant. Couples uncouple in a heartbeat when something gets broken that can't be fixed."

"Yes," he said, "but most trouble starts long before the confrontation. Deceit gradually erodes trust. Secrets cry out, and the injured party starts sensing an unspoken vibe. Sex becomes less frequent or less fulfilling. The breakup doesn't happen until a tipping point is reached, when the benefits no longer exceed costs."

"A relationship isn't a profit-loss statement, Mike. But I get what you're saying. Maybe, over time, one of them stops paying close enough attention. Neglected, the other no longer feels emotionally nourished or reciprocated. Love is giving what you need to get."

They chewed on that thought while chewing on their pasta and *parmigiana*.

Mike continued his theory of disconnection. "They stop listening, doing the little things. Each starts redefining his or her self as a person separate from the partner."

"But it can be a sudden deal-breaker if there's suffocating control and anger, or a physical or emotional threat," she said. "Illusions get shattered. This person is suddenly no longer who you thought they were."

The server interrupted to ask if anything else was needed. They finished their meals quietly, until Mike broke their silence. "Guess we're lucky to be lovers who aren't in love."

Nikki agreed. "That's saved us from having to deal with all kinds of potential conflicts. But maybe you've noticed our dates have become redundant."

"Are you saying I'm too predictable?"

"I have to be honest, Mike. Hormones bring us together each week, not love. Sometimes I feel I'm a socket for your rechargeable battery."

"And I'm a device you borrow to satisfy womanly needs."

"So we've been meeting for the sex, and even that's now become somewhat mechanical."

"When a relationship has been as good as ours, it can't go on forever, Nikki. Maybe we've already slipped. How will it end for us, sudden fire or slow ice?"

"I don't know. We're compatible, but this is no longer going anywhere. Why don't we just walk away now?"

He looked at her as realization clicked, a conclusion reached simultaneously. "The movies and restaurants change, but these weekends keep repeating."

"Exactly."

"So we quit while we're ahead?"

"Why not? We started with a clean slate," she said. "Let's go out the same way, with no negatives and good memories. Win-win and move on."

"You're saying we break up tonight?"

"Yes, Mike. No more contact with each other, so we won't be tempted to come back. We can kick our addiction together. Let's both own this."

"Okay, I'm in, even though we'll both know there will be some withdrawal. I'll miss my uptown girl. What will you do?"

"I want to get out of the city, buy a little house somewhere over in Jersey," she said. "Spring is coming. I could plant a garden, get a dog and a gas grille, maybe put up a bird feeder. I want to settle in a place all my own, slow down, find peace. I think I'll be happier if I fly solo for a while."

"Funny, I've been thinking of breaking free myself, anywhere away from that desk. The job isn't a dead end, but I'm not too excited about the career path. Maybe I should see what's out there."

"Then make a change. Find your dream and pursue it, Mike,

something challenging that gives you room to breathe."

"We made it nine months. That's as long as a pregnancy. If this is our last tango, can I order dessert?"

"Sure. Have whatever you want. When you pick the restaurant, you get the check, remember?" She stood up, reached for her bag and coat. "I've got to go find a cab. Goodbye, Mike."

"Good luck, Nikki."

WE SHOULD
MEET

Prodded by a seductive advertisement on his computer screen, Frank yielded to the lure of an internet dating service for seniors, his photo and credit card data buying thirty days. It took only a few minutes to register the fictitious name *Dreamer* and gain access to the site. He entered his age, height, body type, race, religion, marital and occupational history for the personal profile, writing nothing in response to "What I'm Looking For" or "A Little About Me." Instead, Frank immediately began scrolling pages of women fifty or older living within a twenty mile radius. A mug book of photographs identified each by age, city, and odd pseudonyms: *No Games, Hot Button, Adventurous*. A quick click summoned additional photographs and each woman's detailed self-description, an honor system governing their body type claims. Women identified themselves as slim, athletic, average, or blessed with a few extra pounds. Almost all were divorced with grown children, some still living at home. The rest were widows, or that rare married woman newly separated. A significant percentage wanted to travel, take cruises, and see the world with the right companion. Others hoped to find a man to take them golfing. The computer linked Frank to five new matches a day. No one looked interesting in the first lineup sent to him. While he studied other possibilities, a message from the site advised that *Dream Girl* had chosen him as her "favorite."

As *Dream Girl,* Rachel accessed the site frequently to troll for prospects in her age group. Holding a doctorate degree, she disqualified any male not educated, refusing all widowers and smokers. Fickle and choosy, she had gone through a succession of boyfriends and one-night rejects, telling friends a girl had to suffer endless frogs to find a prince. She did not answer computer flirts, preferring instead to be the initiator. Each session began with a quick check of freshly enrolled subscribers to pounce on any prize newcomer. *Dreamer,* with a pen name similar to hers, immediately caught her eye. An athletic-looking man with nice hair, he stood five-ten, barely meeting her height requirement. At five-seven, Rachel wore three-inch heels to plays, symphonies, and gala balls. A career academic who retired as a small college president, he likely had his own money and would not be chasing hers. A man two years younger, his age fell within her window. Still "eye candy" at sixty-eight, Rachel obsessively maintained the figure that earned employment as a model in her youth. Compulsive about keeping her weight at one-seventeen, she fasted when a pound over, feasted when a pound under. Daily swims kept her fit. If *Dreamer* turned out to be a keeper, she'd make his dreams come true. She sent him a "favorite" alert and continued browsing the site.

Frank never imagined being picked as someone's "favorite" so soon. Flattered, he could not guess what might have attracted a woman to his photo or why she would designate him as her special choice. The *Dream Girl* photo revealed an ageless beauty with straight brown hair, piercing blue eyes, a sexy upper figure showing full cleavage beneath an almost cliché leopard-print top. Before reading her profile, he messaged back, "Why me? How does this work?" Her personal information listed numerous disclaimers, more about what she didn't want in a man than what she was looking for. His designation as her "favorite" became clear when he saw her Doctorate in Business Management and seats on corporate boards. Retired to a luxury condo, she swam in the ocean each day and loved going to the philharmonic. Aptly named, *Dream Girl* sounded too good to be true.

Rachel congratulated herself for being the first to hook this guy. He sounded naïve, admitting his surprise at attracting her attention. She hoped he could carry a conversation above her boredom threshold. He didn't own a motorcycle or a boat, toys she'd enjoyed with previous boyfriends, squeezing into tight leather or sunbathing topless on deck. She had just accepted an all-day first date with a man and his boat, penciled in for Friday. The online service forbade dating more than one match at a time but she ignored the rule. Waiting made no sense when life was so short, shorter for some than for others. She sent *Dreamer* a response. "My name is Rachel. You interest me. We should meet."

Frank now had a name to go with *Dream Girl's* profile and photograph. He messaged a mutual interest in meeting along with his first name and phone number. Her reply said she would call but did not say when. Already eight o'clock, he hoped to hear from her by nine.

Rachel rang an hour later, modulating her voice to soften a heavy New York accent. They traded questions and answers, life histories and commonalities. She told him fate had introduced them, two lapsed Catholics from New Jersey with doctorates, each twice divorced. Frank asked when he could see her.

"Today is Tuesday," she said. "I'm free tomorrow night or next Monday."

"Tomorrow is good. Does protocol require us to meet somewhere public for a drink?"

"It does, Frank. We live fifteen miles apart. The King's Table is halfway."

"Nice choice. Let's forget protocol and take one car. Give me your address and I'll be in front of your building at five."

"What will you be driving?"

"A white Mercedes."

Frank complied with her instructions to call on arrival, and Rachel changed the plan, inviting him upstairs for a glass of wine. He stepped out of the elevator on the seventh floor to find her waiting, a woman with a classic figure, deep tan, and dazzling smile. He joked about meeting her minimum height as she ushered him into a sprawling apartment occupying half the floor, with spectacular views of the Intracoastal and the sea. Windows poured natural Florida light from a southern exposure stretching the full length of the building. Countless artworks complemented expensive furnishings. They poured wine, and sipped it on a breezy balcony above the blue Atlantic. Frank thought he'd be nervous, but Rachel put him at ease with relaxed conversation as they learned more about each other. Her two sons, both professors, lived in distant states; one had a family. She had divorced their late father and a second ex-husband stayed in touch. Without apology, she freely disclosed other men from her past, some remembered with fondness.

Rachel was attracted to Frank and felt comfortable in his presence. Laid-back confidence accentuated his boyish charm. Unlike her previous men, he was not intimidated, relating to her as an equal without patronizing. With refreshing candor and humor, Frank revealed he'd left his first wife for a younger woman only to have the younger woman leave him for a younger man. A good listener, he shared stories with a humble sophistication, and she felt strong chemistry by the time they left for the restaurant. Rejecting The King's Table, they chose a seafood place close to his home, only to find it slammed with July vacationers. She jumped out of the car and persuaded people to move and save two seats for them at the bar, before stepping outside to wave him to the parking lot.

Frank smiled at Rachel's assertiveness in bypassing the waiting crowd. Wine served, food ordered, their positive vibe continued through a discussion of previous loves. Frank admitted to a misplaced, unrequited affection for someone and other romantic mishaps. Rachel's most recent relationship involved cohabitation with a retired executive who lived inland in a golf community. He put in a swimming pool for her but she wasn't a golfer and was never accepted by the women in the club. Trapped, her condo rented, she needed a therapist and anti-depressants before reclaiming her oceanfront home. Frank sensed vulnerability, a puzzling contradiction to her street-smart independence.

Rachel found herself confiding innermost secrets to a stranger she'd met only hours earlier, revealing an abortion between the births of her sons. The pregnancy had coincided with a breakthrough career opportunity. Frank earned her trust with his nonjudgmental ear, a gentleman with the good manners not to ask what her husband thought of the abortion decision, or if he ever knew. When the check came, she insisted on splitting the bill but he put it on his card, telling her she could pay next time. Rachel interpreted his deft move as a sly maneuver to get a second date.

Frank requested a quick stop at his nearby house. He'd been to her home, she should now see his. Rachel did not object, agreeing a woman could learn a lot about a man by seeing how he lived. She praised his proximity to the beach as she entered a tidy dwelling perfectly suited for a man living alone, his study shelved floor-to-ceiling with books. Rachel's eyes lit up when he showed her the large screen-enclosed swimming pool, perfect for winter days too cold for ocean swims. Frank beamed when she said the pool was the right length for swimming laps.

Rachel came close to asking if the pool was heated, or if it could be. The garage contained a matched set of bicycles. She liked everything she saw. He pleased her by driving back leisurely along a scenic river road. She let him walk her to the door of the building without inviting him up. Twilight had not yet faded but she thanked him and said goodnight. Rachel went upstairs, poured herself a nightcap, and watched darkness descend on the ocean as she evaluated this man and their brief time together. She always limited first dates to an early evening with no promise for a second one, the better to eliminate frogs. True princes were patient; she knew she'd hear from him.

Frank phoned the next three days but got no answer and did not leave a message. Thinking he'd struck out, he made one last call on Sunday. Rachel answered, apologizing for her busy weekend and inviting him to stop by for a bite at six. They made sandwiches and talked on her deck until a storm intervened. Wind-driven rain slicked the balcony and drove them inside to her living room. He sat close and made her laugh when he took her hand and told her stormy weather made him dreamy. Her response, an exaggerated sigh, invited a pass, and he made one as Rachel leaned forward, lips parted to receive his kiss. She encouraged his touch and helped when he reached around to unhook her bra, unbuttoning her blouse and freeing her breasts. They necked like teenagers until pausing for breath.

"You're beautiful," he whispered.

"Me, or my parts?"

"The total package, but your parts are nice."

"They're not implants," she said. "I keep myself in shape."

"You make me want you, Rachel. Is that wrong?"

"No. I want you to want me."

"Are we moving too fast?"

"We're okay, but it's getting late. Come back tomorrow night and I'll cook you a salmon dinner." She led him to the door for a final kiss.

"May I bring something?" he asked.

"Surprise me."

Frank drove home entranced. He'd connected with Rachel and tasted her intimacy. She'd reciprocated his affection, affirming he had not gone too far, communicating approval. He could not wait to see her again.

Rachel liked belonging to someone, a woman held, valued, and cared for. Despite his rough edges, Frank had a high potential for grooming. She'd know tomorrow night if he was ready.

Frank showed up with a long-stemmed rose. Rachel looked sensational in a colorful elastic top stretched across her midriff, exposed tan shoulders beneath bright earrings. Resisting prurient impulses, he kissed her hello and complimented her tropical look, a playful island girl mixing margaritas.

Happy to be cooking a meal for a man again, Rachel enjoyed watching him eat. Frank was an instant answer to loneliness, a paradox for a woman at peace in her own company. After he helped her clean up, they addressed a different hunger in the kitchen until she took his hand and led him to her bedroom.

Worried what Rachel might think if he declined, Frank became a reluctant collaborator on just their third date. Ignoring his awkwardness, she took control, touching, learning, teaching, giving and taking pleasure. He slept intermittently until a red sun rose from a gray sea.

Rachel nuzzled the man in her bed as if mothering a sleeping child. She had offered sex sooner rather than later to find out if Frank was functional. His lovemaking, patient and unhurried, removed all doubt as he let her direct their choreography.

Now a couple, they walked the beach as morning-after lovers. Rachel apologized for a diminished libido from the anti-depressant she'd recently stopped taking. She would need months to wean herself from the side effects. Frank had awakened her appetite; she would try to accommodate his. He vowed it wouldn't be a problem. Rachel confided daily medications controlled her blood pressure and Valium helped her sleep. He felt protective, more so after learning her father had abandoned her mother when Rachel was eleven years old. Caregiver to a shattered parent, she could not forgive a father gone to live with another woman, hating and loving him at the same time. Her therapist told her the ordeal left her incapable of trusting any man. Frank countered with a confession about his own dysfunctional family, combative parents who drowned all familial love with incessant conflict, driving him away.

The new couple became inseparable through a blissful summer, Frank spending weekdays at the condo, Rachel visiting his house on weekends for bicycling, takeout by the pool, naked swims in the dark. She bought two season subscriptions to the symphony an hour away and introduced him to classical music. He lost weight eating the healthier foods she cooked, and purchased new clothing and a tuxedo for a formal gala ball, where Rachel's stunning gown drew stares and smiles of approval. She initiated sex a few mornings a week, girl on top. At night they watched "Jeopardy," "Wheel of Fortune," and classic movies, Frank massaging her back and legs until she fell asleep. At her beach, they would read beneath an umbrella and body surf in the sea, Rachel the stronger swimmer. Retreating to the condo, they'd rinse off, swim in the pool, and relax in the heated Jacuzzi before going upstairs to shower together. Ocean temperatures stayed warm through October.

When cooler weather arrived, Frank bought a heater for his

pool, writing off the cost as an investment in property value. Rachel visited more frequently, a topless mermaid swimming endless laps as Frank watched. He entertained her with stories, many from his tenure as a college president, where he resolved conflicts with trustees, faculty and students. Rachel wanted to pay half the cost of the heat pump, but he let her buy a lamp and table and replaced an uncomfortable living room couch with a cozy sectional she helped pick out.

They spent the Christmas holidays at Frank's house and became a popular couple at parties thrown by her friends. By January, Rachel had moved in with Frank and leased her condo for the month of February. He helped her remove clothes from closets and clean the unit. She spent afternoons by his pool, swimming, reading, working Sudoku puzzles, phoning managers of two rental properties she owned, one a townhouse in California. She asked Frank if he would consider selling their four properties, including his home, to combine assets and buy a luxury house on the beach. Frank said he would, for the right home in the right location. This tentative agreement led to appointments with realtors but introduced new pressure.

Frank noticed Rachel's increased irritability with restaurant servers and people in general. She suffered panic attacks whenever they were stuck in traffic, demanding he take the nearest escape route. She had zero tolerance for any communication remotely resembling criticism. Aware of a shift in their balance of power, Frank saw Rachel taking more control. They were evolving but not in a good way.

Rachel had her own doubts. Approaching commitment, she felt indecision rooted in previous, failed relationships. Frank had admitted to a strong authority complex. He might become controlling and judgmental, not the man she thought he was. She feared being taken for granted, a woman no longer valued. His feelings for her could change. Men always changed.

Frank asked her to ignore his over-tipping in restaurants. The more she abused servers, the more he tipped. Rachel's affections seemed to diminish, with less kissing and fewer invitations for sex. Their plans to buy a house together shelved, he walked on eggshells to avoid upsetting her or their fragile relationship. When he teased about her missing pubic hair, she said most men liked it that way, reducing Frank to just another in a long line of boyfriends.

Rachel worried Frank's upbringing bred negativity. She'd abandoned friends for him. He didn't understand what she had to deal with. His life was uncomplicated and carefree. His excusing poor service in restaurants seemed to mock her. She needed him to stand tall, take charge, make the advances when he wanted sex so she wouldn't have to guess. Growing anxiety led to thoughts of seeing her therapist.

In March, they drove five hundred miles to visit her son and grandchildren. The six-year-old girl and four-year-old boy were unruly. Both parents had careers, and blamed the hyperactive misbehavior of their children on poorly supervised day care. Rachel clearly disliked her grandchildren, letting her son know she would not involve herself in correcting them, expressing disapproval of how they were being raised. He said he no longer wanted her around his kids. Her subsequent silent withdrawal infuriated her son, causing him to drink until he exploded in rage, accusing his mother of ruining his life, calling her a borderline psychotic. Frank quickly packed the car to get them out of there. The son pursued, banging on the passenger window, shouting profanities and threats, insisting he never wanted to see his mother again. They drove all night without stopping, arriving at his house at dawn. Frank gave consolation the entire way, siding with Rachel, reminding her nothing excused her son's actions. But he saw cracks in her self-esteem, already evident in her obsession with facial wrinkles and denials of self-worth, doubt replacing narcissism. The ordeal brought them closer, two wronged victims against the world.

The cease-fire was short-lived. Easter brought warm days and a small army of renters to occupy her building's empty units. Rachel went to war with all of them, over water dripped in the elevator, unlocked gates, and late night parties on the pool deck. Unit owners lived in other states, and she roused them from sleep with loud, ranting phone calls. Frank tried to calm her, volunteering to represent her in all dealings with the association board. When an attorney served her with a 'cease and desist' letter, Rachel spun into deep depression. They had ruined her peace, spoiled enjoyment of her home. She wanted to sell the condo. He tried to downplay the lawyer's letter as a maneuver designed to cover his client's negligence. She needed to be alone but also wanted him to stay. Frank could not grant both requests. Suspecting her shutdown a result from re-taking anti-depressants, he now suffered the same frustration expressed by her son. They both had violated her fragile trust. The word "love" had never been uttered by either of them, but he loved Rachel enough to set her free if that would relieve her stress. Frank ached to hold and comfort her but something had broken that couldn't be fixed. He asked her what she wanted from him.

"Nothing. I'll never be happy," she answered.

"Rachel, you have beauty, physical health, properties worth millions, a six figure income, a man who adores you. What's missing?"

"Don't judge me. I can't give you what you need."

"I need whatever you can give. It just has to be consistent," he said.

"I can't give you happiness. I can't even give it to myself."

"Then I must be the problem. Should I pack my things and bring your stuff back in the morning?"

"Yes."

The next day, it took numerous trips from car to elevator to return her possessions. As he stacked clothing on her bed, Frank hoped Rachel would communicate a change of heart, but she never looked at him. Beaten, Frank left. They had lasted a year.

Two months passed without a phone call or email. He re-subscribed to the dating site. Days later, the computer matched him with *Mermaid*. Under a new fictitious name, new photographs and fresh disclaimers about what she didn't need in a man, it was Rachel.

She sent Frank a message.

It said "We should meet."

GUNS

Our toys were guns. Impersonating cowboys, we wore hats and gun belts with pearl-handled cap pistols. Later, we became child soldiers in military clothing, carrying canteens and authentic-looking guns. Mine, a black plastic replica of a forty-five semi-automatic, came with a white military police holster and ten wooden bullets in a spring-loaded magazine. I'd acquired it as a Christmas gift from my grandparents.

The combat battleground a mile from our neighborhood featured dense foliage, a shallow creek, and a steep clay hill in a place we called The End of the World. The war game required each of us to become the enemy of every other. A ten minute truce allowed combatants to scatter. Then, every boy for himself, we waited in ambush or hunted each other down, never dreaming kids like us would someday be sent to Asian jungles to wage real war with real guns.

Toy guns outgrown, I filled my time with a bicycle and a route delivering afternoon and Sunday morning newspapers. Fridays required getting off the bike to receive collections from customers, most warm and friendly but some cold and distant. Both types lived down the street in the Lyle household. Amy, a sweet mother of two towheaded boys and husband Jimmy, a brooding town cop. Mrs. Lyle always had a kind word and sometimes warm cookies or a slice of cake when she made her weekly payment.

One Friday, I knocked on their screen door and saw my first real gun. Jimmy Lyle sat at the kitchen table cleaning his service weapon and stared at me as he passed it from one hand to the other. When I knocked a second time, he said I'd have to come back later to get my money.

Officer Jimmy did not like kids and we did not like him, our mutual dislike growing each year. Boots and gun belt leather creaked when he strutted past stores in our two stoplight town. Popping out of his patrol car with a sneer, he dispersed high school kids hanging out at parks and ball fields or in front of Woolworth's, threatening all of us with arrest for loitering.

In our senior year, Artie Atkinson, always clowning, brought a real gun to school in the precisely cut-out pages of a book, and showed it off at lunch. Later, Officer Lyle burst into Chemistry class to get the gun and take Artie, slapping on the cuffs and dragging him out. We crowded lab tables by the windows to watch them cross the front lawn. Artie was kicked and shoved all the way to the car and knocked down whenever he tried to stand, Lyle pushing him into the back seat headfirst.

Weekend and summer nights, couples parked in a secluded area near an abandoned stock car track on the edge of town. Officer Lyle policed them by surprise, rolling up with lights and engine off so he could shine a flashlight on backseat lovers. One night we set him up, three guys innocently waiting in Danny Tomlin's car. The officer beamed his light on our faces and asked if we had beer in the vehicle. Our guilty expressions invited his futile search as he belittled us for not having dates. Lyle's investigation gave two buddies hiding nearby enough time to crawl on their bellies and let the air out of the patrol car's rear tires. We picked them up on our way back to the main road.

That autumn, I enrolled in a commuter college twenty miles away. I met a girl who lived farther out, and took her to a movie theatre in her town. I was sitting on the end of a row when Jimmy Lyle passed by, holding hands with a blonde. She was the kind of woman men looked at, one who wanted them to look. Sitting four rows ahead, the two silhouettes kissed frequently. When the movie ended, I got my date out of there before Jimmy could see me.

Two weeks later, I learned Amy Lyle had been killed. She'd gone into their bedroom to get help with a necklace clasp and startled Jimmy as he was loading his gun to go on shift. Startled, he turned and the gun went off, putting a bullet through her heart.

They ruled the shooting accidental.

EURO SKY HOP

The ancient aircraft wobbled on takeoff, its engines coughing and straining to gain altitude as the flight over the English Channel threatened a one-way ticket to eternity. Passengers who had been laughing and shouting in many languages now sat frozen in silence, their white knuckles squeezing armrests. The plane had no flight attendant or crew, only a suspect pilot and a threadbare cabin. I could see the headline in the newspaper back home, "Two high school teachers killed in plane crash, Tom Wade, forty-one, Kay Brandt, twenty-seven."

Eleven months earlier, high school coaches returning from summer vacation greeted each other with playful insults. The athletic director announced a staff addition. "We've hired a girls' volleyball coach who will teach art and German, a cute hippie who doesn't shave her legs. Too young for you, Wade, so stay away."

His warning became a challenge to a divorced loner reduced to refusing blind dates suggested by my colleagues' wives. They introduced the new hire at the morning faculty meeting. Still in her twenties, with sturdy build and honey-blonde hair, she wore a print dress and no makeup. Her sunshine smile lit the room and beckoned my lost youth. In a used book store that afternoon, I was inspired to buy two dozen hard cover novels written in

German, ten dollars for the carton. Each day, I placed a single volume in her mail box, saving the last book to present to her in person. I found Miss Kay Brandt seated in the faculty lounge with two male coaches ridiculing her unshaved legs. After they left, I handed her the final gift.

"The secret book donor reveals himself!" she exclaimed. "Where did you find them?"

"In a dusty bookstore downtown. I think your legs are fine without the razor."

"Now you're hitting on me. You sexist coaches are all alike."

"You wrongly accuse. Female body hair is delightfully European. When I retire, I'm moving to a Greek isle to find the woman on the raisin box."

"You should've come forward sooner," she said. "You're either a coward or a guy who plays games."

"Maybe I'm both."

She stood up. "I've got to go teach class. Stop by the gym after school. You can observe our volleyball match and critique my coaching."

Shrieks and yells from shrill-voiced competitors communicated volleyball's intensity as a spirited Coach Brandt shouted encouragement. Her team dropped the first game but came back in the next two to win a close match. She sent her girls to the showers and glowed with victory as I extended my hand in congratulations.

"Nice job, coach. Your strategic adjustments made the difference."

"I just yelled louder after we lost the first game," she said.

"Your kids heard you. Coaching golf is easier. I'm prohibited from talking to our boys during matches."

She grew serious. "Thanks for being here. Listen, a bunch of teachers meet at the Mexican restaurant near the airport every

Thursday night for beers and dancing. Come join us."

"Maybe I'll stop by to help you celebrate your win."

I changed my mind more than once before going. The bar was rocking when I arrived, couples gyrating to recorded dance music. Alone and awkward, I felt relieved when I spotted Kay and she motioned me to her group. They were all first-year teachers who had bonded during district orientation, their introductions a blur of names until she presented the man she was with.

"Tom, this is my friend Dirk Mueller. Dirk, I'd like you to meet a teacher from my school, Tom Wade. Dirk is from Germany."

My heart sank. I shook hands with a virile young man who smiled a lot but didn't say much. She had not introduced Dirk as her boyfriend but clearly he was. Her deft invitation to the night-spot let me know she was already taken, I could forget pursuing her.

"Dirk and I were just heading to the dance floor. When we come back, I'll be asking you to dance with me."

I took satisfaction watching Dirk's stiff, awkward spasms beside Kay's liquid, exotic movements. When it was my turn, I caught the music's beat with steps imitating Kay's, earning her bemused smile.

I returned her to her man, finished my beer, said goodnight and left the bar. A week later, after more internal debate, I was back, ignoring inner cautions to stay away.

The script repeated, week after week. I'd make polite conver-sation, acknowledge Dirk, borrow his woman for a ten minute dance and make an early exit, vowing to quit my role as backup dance partner, only to return to the bar the following Thursday.

Week six: After dancing with Kay, I was pulled back on the floor by a woman my age, someone I'd dated years earlier when she was a fellow faculty member. Back then, she'd moonlighted as a model, making weekend trips to the Bahamas to do photo shoots promoting suntan lotion. We danced a long set with Kay watching. When the music stopped, Kay and her date were gone. I found her waiting outside in the parking lot, leaning against her car.

"Where's Dirk?" I asked.

"He's returning to Germany on an early flight." Her tone sounded tired. "We said our goodbyes."

"Why are you standing here?"

"I'm low on gas. I need you to follow me 'til I get over the bridge."

I stayed on her bumper as she took a meandering route across the city. Flashing lights stopped us at a train crossing, Kay first in line at the gate. As freight cars rattled by, she got out of her car and came to my window, leaning in with a serious kiss and asking for my phone number. When I got home, the phone rang. She said "thanks," and hung up.

On Sunday night, she called again.

"Mr. Wade, what are you doing?"

"I'm stuffing old shirts in a plastic bag to give to the needy."

"Can I pick out a couple?"

"Sure. When?"

"Right now. You know where I live."

Fifteen years earlier, I'd rented an apartment down the street from her tiny cinder block duplex. She answered the door in a low-cut sundress, inviting me to sit down while she examined the shirts. She chose two with alligator logos and, dropping her top, pulled the navy one over her head.

"It fits perfectly," she said.

"That shirt has tiny holes," I warned. "You can't wear it to school."

She leaned forward and thanked me with a kiss longer and more serious than the first one three nights earlier, asking, "Are you pursuing me, Mr. Wade?"

"Yes," I answered. "Is it obvious?"

"It's obvious you hope to become my lover."

"Are you accepting applications?"

"I'll give yours careful consideration."

"When do I find out?"

"Tonight, after your interview. It might take hours."

She whispered the questions in German, my non-verbal answers a cause of sleep deprivation in her small bed. In the morning, she smiled in the shower, eyes closed above her freckle-faced overbite as streams of water splashed wet, beautiful curves.

Kay favored impulsive, spur-of-the-moment dates, spontaneous competitions in bowling or tennis where she belittled my form. Walks on the beach were reserved for the coldest nights in freezing winds, field trips to view lighted, oceanfront mansions. Once we stood in a howling wind watching millionaires party with their backs to the giant windows, secretly patting each other's rumps. I suffered long bike rides over tall bridges without complaint. My key to the gym allowed Sunday morning basketball games where her rule required me to shoot only with my left hand. Indoors, Kay loved Scrabble, playing expertly at a quick pace, a woman who hated losing.

She insisted on paying her own way. If I grabbed a restaurant check, she'd buy groceries for our next dinner. My home was far too big for her. Kay did not understand the collections of books, vinyl records, antique golf clubs, old postcards and autographed baseballs. None of it made sense to a woman who could fit all her worldly possessions in a Ford Escort. My house became an issue when she refused to spend the night there. Equally stubborn, I frequently rejected the duplex and her single bed to sleep in my own.

Over Christmas break we tried a weekend in Charleston, exploring the city by day and playing Scrabble at night. The weather was cold, causing fatigue, disappointment, and petty irritations. In February we drove three hours to meet her parents, her mother welcoming but her father stern and distant. We were assigned separate bedrooms in a sprawling home with a canal out back and a huge yacht moored to a dock, ready for cruises on the Gulf. A German-American success story, the family banked steady revenue from diverse businesses. Kay seemed unusually quiet on the trip home.

"What's the matter?" I asked.

"I've been wondering why you got a vasectomy."

"My ex-wife requested it."

"Can it be reversed?"

"Not easily. There are no guarantees."

"You never wanted kids?"

"I invested too much energy in other people's kids. And, in case you haven't noticed, teachers don't make a whole lot of money."

Raising eyebrows with our age-disparate relationship, I had also failed an important test. If we weren't right for one another, the disqualifying issue could have been her wish to someday have children. One of her sisters had already birthed three, obeying a family mandate to marry and produce grandchildren.

Spring Break brought a happier seventeen-hour drive to New York City to see her best friend. Our lone disagreement was over a scheduled trip to Europe she'd called off. Driving home on long stretches of interstate, I pouted about her rescinded invitation. Kay broke a long silence in one of the Carolinas.

"I had a nice time. I'm glad we got along so well in front of my friends."

"We've mellowed," I said. "Quarreling tires us out."

"Why are we still together?" she asked.

"I don't know. Maybe we fight because the sex is so great when we make up."

"I should take you with me to Europe after all."

"I thought you cut me out so you could meet up with Dirk."

"No, I won't be seeing him again. I want to show you the university in Freiburg where I spent two wonderful years."

We planned the trip as the school year wound down, buying backpacks to eliminate suitcases. Kay tied extra handles with a length of rope and found fanny packs for passports and travelers checks. We picked out sturdy walking shoes, layers of clothing, and rain gear. The itinerary, loose and flexible, would rely on bed and breakfasts and cheap hotels. The airline tickets earned a bonus rental car for a week, pickup and return at the Frankfurt airport.

A new crisis nearly cancelled everything. Kay's teaching status had been probationary. The principal informed her she would not be back. He gave the standard excuses, budget cuts and shifting numbers, but avoided specifics. A female administrator had spoken to her about presenting a more professional, ladylike appearance. And her school keys, misplaced during a Saturday foreign language festival, were never found, a problem as serious as a police officer losing a gun. Dating an older faculty member could have sealed her fate.

We didn't flaunt the relationship but refused to hide. Word got out the first time we were spotted in public. My fellow coaches never mentioned Kay, their silence a subtle disapproval. I felt responsible. My job was never at risk but Kay did not have tenure. I had to do something. An old friend of mine in the county administrative hierarchy helped her land a teaching job in a city thirty miles away. We found a rental house for her there just before our departure to Europe.

When the plane landed in Frankfurt, we agreed Kay would

do all the driving, a reverse of our car trips in the States. She knew the roads and how to get where we were going. I felt lucky to be traveling with a woman who spoke fluent German. We drove to Heidelberg, visited the castle, and slept off jet lag in an immaculate room.

Europe brought us closer. Kay drove safely in the right lane on the autobahn to Munich. We parked near the city center beside a brewery as big as a refinery, and marveled at medieval gates, beer gardens, and steep roofs with ornate gables. At nightfall, we left Bavaria for Vienna. We did not know Germany's factories had just been shut down, a two-week summer holiday with a Friday night sendoff for hundreds of thousands of workers, most of them traveling on the same road to the Balkans. Traffic on the autobahn halted. After inching along for miles, we were lucky to find a parking spot at a rest stop. With no choice but to sleep in the little Renault, we woke to vandalized windshield wipers and a bent radio antennae.

Traffic thinned when most of the drivers exited south toward their homelands. We reached Vienna, parked the car, and hopped a bus. Kay scored a nice room overlooking the outdoor market and a pair of tickets to a Saturday matinee performance of "Cats." Our seats were in a corner of the highest balcony, where I kept nodding off. Peaceful harmony continued until Monday, when a tortuous ride back through the Austrian Alps drew my complaint.

"Do we have to drive so fast? I get nervous when you're driving one-handed and pointing at the scenery."

"You always have to criticize," she said, her defiant foot pressing the gas pedal.

"I have no choice when my life is in danger."

"I'm driving at normal speed. What's your problem?"

"I've been watching the speedometer, trying to convert

the kilometers. This highway isn't straight like the one in Germany."

The car slowed slightly, and she pouted in silence all the way to Feldkirch. We parked and toured the town separately. Later, I found her standing by a noisy green river, in tears. She refused to speak, and left no doubt I was the cause.

"Something I said?" I asked.

"People looking at us must see a girl needing a father figure," she sniffed.

"Maybe they see a lustful old man with prurient interests."

"Sometimes I wish I'd met you later in my life."

"And I wish I'd met you sooner in mine."

"It's been a hopeless match since sooner met later."

"Now we're a couple in limbo. Look," I said, "maybe we should split up and meet back at the airport on the day we fly home. I can manage by myself. Everybody over here speaks English."

Nearby, at a picnic table, a huge man eating a huge sandwich looked at us in disgust, his sympathies clearly with the crying young woman. The rushing river remained neutral as she considered and rejected my idea

"I'll be okay. Let's go."

She took us to the art museums in Basel, then on to Freiburg, a city where she'd lived and studied. We had supper, purchased wine and chocolates, and walked through the town to her old dorm. There, two young women remembered her with joyful hugs.

"Isn't this great? We can spend the night on couches in the reception area."

I said, "No, Let's go check in somewhere."

"It's okay to stay here," she insisted. "People do it all the time."

"Were we invited?"

"No, but it won't be a problem."

"I'll go wait in the car."

Her visit took a half-hour. She returned and explained we'd have to go into the country to find a bed and breakfast. We stopped at several, but Kay came back from each saying the price was too high. Upset, she pulled off the road and announced we'd be spending the night in the car. I got out to walk off my own anger and slammed the door behind me.

Several hundred yards down the road, I came to a bridge over a deep ravine, a good vantage point for watching a beautiful sunset. Down below, a farmhouse cookout emitted grilled cooking scents and high volume classic American rock music. I recognized an old Dell Shannon tune, and sang along at the top of my voice, "My little run-run-run-run runaway…"

The guy at the grill looked up and I waved, yelling "American!" and pointing at my chest.

He gestured toward the food and shouted, "Come down… we party!"

I ran back to the car where Kay was moping. I grabbed the wine and chocolates and said, "I just got us invited to a party. Join me if you like." She followed down the unpaved road to the house, where a family was celebrating getting the hay in. Two couples and an elderly patriarch led us inside. Half the building was a barn with cows. We sat down at a huge wooden table in a spotless kitchen, plenty of food for everyone, tasty meat and salad, hot noodles and cold beer, our warm wine and chocolates for dessert.

The elder sat at the head of the table, a man with a barrel chest and several gold teeth. Our candy prompted his story about the American army that passed through their valley during the war, giving out Hersey bars. Kay, seated on his right, translated. The party went on for hours. At one point the old guy put his arm around her and said, "You and me, we make babies?"

Hearty laughter toasted a World War II survivor still prolific and trolling for sex. For a brief moment, I wished I could make babies. Kay never looked happier or more beautiful.

We returned the car in Frankfurt and took a bus to the office of a friend of her parents. The man hugged Kay and insisted we go to his home for dinner, calling ahead to have his wife meet us at the train station. The house, modest on the outside, was opulent inside with a swimming pool in the basement. After the meal, our host tapped a small keg of beer and we retired to a sitting room for suds and stories. He was keenly interested when Kay mentioned my collections, particularly the baseball trading cards, and took me to his study.

He brought out a video. "Have you seen *Das Boot*?"

"Yes, with English subtitles," I answered. "The movie about a German U-boat captain."

"Better without subtitles. I watch it again and again."

He snapped the movie into a recorder, bringing it to life on a television screen, and reached to a bookshelf for a small box containing a set of cards. With a glint in his eye, my host opened it to reveal a collection of small color prints of Hitler, red swastika flags in every scene, maybe fifty cards in all. As we examined each, the man left no doubt he treasured his collection of Fuhrer images.

"I got these from my grandfather," he said, smiling through rimless spectacles. "What do you think?"

I was thinking about the movie where Laurence Olivier plays a Nazi dentist in Brazil doing torture extractions of Dustin Hoffman's teeth. "They must be rare," I said.

"Yes, priceless."

I didn't tell Kay about this scary show and tell until we were alone at the basement pool the next morning. She made no comment as she swam sensual naked laps in water too cold for me. She reprimanded my hungry look when she hoisted herself out.

"Don't get any ideas," she warned. "These people like you, but they're close with my parents. You should never have asked them if we could stay a second night."

"Blame the beer. Why did they put us in the same room in one bed?"

"They were being polite. We'll reciprocate by abstaining. Tonight, we're taking them out to dinner."

We thanked our hosts and took the train back to Frankfurt. Kay stashed me at an outdoor table with a pastry and a *USA Today* newspaper while she went exploring. When she returned, I asked, "When are we taking the train to Amsterdam?"

"We're not. I found this inexpensive bus trip with a short flight that will have us in London by tonight. It looks comfortable, with tables so we can play cards."

"Euro Sky Hop" sounded promising. I readily agreed to the change in plans.

Seven hours later, bracing for death on a wheezing, vibrating plane, I silently promised if Kay and I survived, I'd do the right thing and set her free. She probably had similar thoughts, waiting for the right moment. I vowed to accommodate her until our return to America.

The aircraft landed safely. Kay had booked an affordable high-ceilinged room in London University housing, breakfast included. We walked the city and found a small magnetic scrabble game in a toy store. At a musical celebrating American Blues, Kay shocked the theatre by dancing in the aisle. Later, we both danced in a pub with a knockoff Joe Cocker band. Patrons stared at us with dark looks as they drained their pints. When Kay ordered ours, the bartender asked if we hadn't already had enough. Violating protocol, we danced until the pub closed.

In the morning, a train took us to Cambridge for our last six days. We rented a sunny room in a bed and breakfast with bikes for the week, pedaling to the American World War II cemetery outside town. Restored, we saw a college play, a puppet show on the common, and the Cathedral at Ely, shooting eight-ball every night in a local watering spot. We were happy, maybe because the end was now so near.

In London, we hiked from the train station to the "Euro Sky Hop" connection and the dreaded flight back to the continent. Lucky to land safely a second time, we calmed our nerves on the bus to Frankfurt. Over dinner, Kay suggested spending the night at the airport instead of renting a room. This would preclude checkout hassles and worries about early morning transportation. I did not argue.

Surprise, they locked the airport concourses at night and herded a sinister overnight crowd into a central waiting area. Strange characters kept me awake all night while Kay slept on my shoulder. At dawn, we learned a woman in labor had diverted our plane before it left America, causing a six hour delay in our flight home. Backpacks carried on our incoming flight now had to be checked as luggage. The pilot announced our crowded flight would take a short cut over France and the Atlantic to make up time.

Separated from each other by an aisle, Kay's seat one row back, we handed the small magnetic Scrabble board back and forth. I was three points behind when my last tile scored a two-point word, leaving Kay with one subtracted point, ending our game in a tie. People pointed at windows. Thousands of feet below, an emerald sea border surrounded the hook of Bermuda.

Landed in Orlando, we stood in separate customs lines, our silence continuing on the shuttle bus and in my car. We drove directly to Kay's new home. After retrieving her backpack, I apologized.

"I'm sorry I was such a jerk over there."

"I behaved just as badly."

"Sometimes I think we'd both rather be right than be loved."

"Love?" she asked, startled by the word.

"Sorry. We're too stubborn for love."

"Maybe we need a vacation from each other, time to think."

And time for her new house and new job in a new city, maybe a new man, someone younger who could give her babies. I would have time to embrace middle age. Ready to suggest we simply move on, I sensed she already had.

I heard myself say, "Yeah, time apart, we should do that."

"Let's keep in touch," she said.

We both knew we wouldn't.

THE BOY

A chain link fence separated the Catholic orphanage from the Ford dealership next door. Each afternoon, the boy stood at the metal barrier in the same spot, isolated from other captive children playing on the grounds behind him, staring at rows of shiny cars and the people who came to buy them. A brisk October wind snapped plastic pennants strung above the showroom as dead leaves skipped across the asphalt. Near the highway entrance, the stiff breeze stretched an enormous American flag, urging people to buy a car as an act of patriotism.

Sitting in his glass cubicle a hundred yards away, Bobby Quinn studied the boy. The kid first caught his eye weeks earlier, while he was on the lot selling a used Fiesta to a senior citizen. The same questions kept repeating: The boy's name and age; how he was orphaned; why he chose to be a loner; if shattered hopes brought tears when he lay awake at night. Observing this lonely child, the salesman saw himself at age nine, a boy who watched and waited day after day for a father who never came home, leaving him to grow up without one.

Bobby Quinn wanted to approach the boy and talk to him but knew he shouldn't. On one pretext or another, he'd made numerous trips out to that part of the lot to tinker with cars near the fence. Raising hoods, changing the vinyl price numbers on the windows, opening doors to air out interiors, tying helium-filled balloons to windshield wipers, he'd gotten close enough to see the child's haunting blue eyes and the frayed cuffs on his too-large denim jacket.

A young couple needing help knocked on his office window. He learned they were commuting to two jobs in one vehicle and would purchase a second car if he could win their trust. Convinced he was on their side, they let Bobby put them into a nice Fusion, decent mileage, good condition, single owner. The price and low payments financed over thirty-six months fit their budget. The deal provided a great start to his Friday afternoon, one more car sold with the boy watching. Another tally for the dealership's top closer, first place in both new and used car sales, a magician who could move inventory in a slow economy. Steady commissions had made it possible for Bobby and his wife Nita to move into a new home. Their sweet life lacked nothing — except the ability to have children.

Years earlier, a surgical procedure saved Nita's life but left her barren. Consoling each other, they vowed to be thankful for God's blessings. Committed to their Catholic faith, attending Mass every Sunday, they socialized only on Saturday nights with a circle of couples in private homes or at a local tavern. The other men envied Bobby for his beautiful wife. A respected human resources manager, Nita made him proud, tracking their money and savings so they could pay down the mortgage and buy furniture and a screened enclosure for the patio. Both drove new Ford Taurus sedans, low-cost demos Bobby traded for each year. Evenings and weekends, the blissful couple held hands on walks through their subdivision, deeply in love, living the American dream.

Years at the dealership earned Bobby the luxury of repeat

customers. His smooth style and strategic corner office gave him an edge in racking up sales, enough to hand off prospective buyers of any used cars not Fords. Letting other salesmen close the deals and complete the paperwork allowed him to stay loyal to the brand and share the wealth. Generosity is its own reward, Nita would say. He already had all the business he could handle, elderly people looking for something safe and sensible, families wanting sport utility vehicles, playboys and playgirls seeking classy Mustangs, tough macho guys claiming huge pickup trucks. In negotiations, Bobby had a way of getting to a dollar number that let everybody win, banks included.

He owed his success to an inner peace and confidence inspired by Nita. Winning her heart made him a rich man who could not imagine life without her. She'd grown more beautiful each year, a striking, dark-haired woman with brown eyes, laughing smile, and unconditional love for her husband. With their marriage secure, he believed an adoption could give her the child she always wanted.

On Monday, his day off, Bobby drove to the dealership but parked at the orphanage instead. He'd been deeply moved by his priest's homily during Mass, a request for prayers to end the suffering of innocent children victimized by terror and war, the final words reminding worshipers *the world will be saved one child at a time.* Bobby felt the message had been sent directly from God to him, in response to his persistent thoughts about coming to the boy's rescue. He had not yet pitched the idea to Nita, thinking it better to wait until he'd done the research. If they qualified, he was sure she'd agree.

They could give the child a good home with his own room, raise him and teach him everything he needed to know. Bobby would help the boy with homework, play catch in the backyard, and coach his Little League team. Life would be complete if they could open their hearts and believe in the dream.

The century-old stone masonry of the main building gave the orphanage the look of an aging prison. A secretary ushered him into Sister Alicia's plain, sun-drenched office, a space as immaculate as the stiff white habit framing her rimless glasses and pale skin. A polished hardwood floor gleamed beneath large portraits of Jesus and the Virgin Mary. He expected muted sounds from children in a distant part of the building but heard only the loud ticking of a clock. A black rotary dial telephone occupied a corner of the bare wooden desk. The nun rose and extended her hand, motioning him to sit in the chair opposite.

"How may we help you?"

"My name is Robert Quinn. I work next door at the car dealership. I've come to ask about your adoption procedures and to learn the name and age of the boy who stands by our fence."

"Thank you for coming. Adoption is a legal process handled by courts, not by us. We only place children, when and if we can. I cannot reveal his name, but the boy you refer to is nine years old. He is a special case."

"How special?"

"The child suffered severe physical abuse in his early years, before enduring a series of foster homes. He has retreated into himself and become withdrawn. Given his detachment and fragility, it will be difficult for us to place him."

"Isn't an orphan better off living in a home with a loving family?"

"We rarely see orphans. Most of our children, like this one, have at least one living parent, a legal status complicating placement. Some of them will be with us until they reach the age of consent."

Bobby grew anxious. People usually warmed to him, but Sister Alicia had yet to crack a smile, offering little encouragement.

Sensing rejection, he made his pitch.

"Sister, my wife and I are good practicing Catholics, as Father Dolan over at Queen of Peace can attest. We're financially secure, both of us have good jobs, and we just moved into a new home in a neighborhood with a good school. Are we not the quality people you're looking for?"

"We don't know. You and your wife will have to be interviewed separately and together with a counselor coming to your home. Her employment could be disqualifying. An optimum environment for the boy would require a stay-at-home parent with no other children. Both of you would need training in parenting skills even before meeting the child."

"Are you saying we have a chance?"

"Mr. Quinn, we never say 'never.' Our children are secure in this institution but the right home is always a better option. It is possible you could meet our strict requirements for placement. But this child may not be able to bond with you and your wife in ways you might expect. With that understanding, if you still wish to submit an application, my secretary can give you the forms."

Sister Alicia's brow furrowed as she covered each point, betraying no emotion. At least she had opened the door a crack. One would think she'd be overjoyed at the possibility one of these unclaimed children might be wanted and loved. Bobby stood, thanked her and picked up the paperwork as he left the building.

Getting into his car, he looked toward the edge of the property. The boy stood there at the fence in his usual place. Driving home, he decided he would sit down with Nita after Mass on Sunday, to learn what she thought of the idea.

Over the next five days he felt distracted, mentally rehearsing the conversation at work, managing to complete multiple sales of new vehicles while the boy watched from his post. Bobby wondered if the children would be kept indoors once the weather grew colder. Saturday was Halloween, but these kids would not be out trick-or-treating.

Their friends decided against the weekly Saturday night party so the couples could stay home and pass out candy. Nita delighted in seeing the costumed children coming to the door. Bobby saw her joy as a favorable sign for the talk he had planned. At Mass the next morning, he realized Sunday had fallen on All Saints Day, a holy day of obligation to commemorate all souls beatified in heaven, saints or not. Father Dolan dedicated the Feast of All Saints to those who died in a state of grace and closed with *blessed are the meek, for they will inherit the earth.*

Routinely, Bobby and Nita came home from Mass and sat down for a brunch while deciding how to spend their one full day of the week together. In good weather, they'd plan something outdoors or a short trip somewhere for an adventure. Stormy Sundays provided an excuse to go back to bed, for an afternoon of watching old classic movies and making love. On this day, it began raining while they were eating. Bobby cleared the table and asked his wife to remain seated.

"Nita, there's this little boy I see every day at work, standing by the orphanage fence. He's gotten into my head, and my heart is telling me we should do something. I've been thinking he could be the child we've never been able to have. This is our opportunity. We could welcome him into our home, experience the one thing missing in our lives."

He went on to describe the boy and what he'd been able to learn about him from Sister Alicia, including every negative issue against his proposal. When he saw tears well in Nita's eyes, he interpreted her emotion as happiness. She did not speak until he had finished.

"The idea of our adopting this boy shows compassion, Bobby, every warm quality I love about you. With all my heart, I want to say yes to what you're asking, but I can't. Accepting a child in our lives is something I cannot do, something we should not do."

Her answer stunned him. "Why? I thought we always planned to adopt a child someday."

"Once we knew I couldn't have children, we never talked about it. Maybe we should have. I accepted God's plan for me a long time ago and moved on. He gave me you and our life together. That's everything I need, all I ever *will* need."

"Nita, if you could just come down to the lot on Saturday and see him, you'd feel the same way I do. I think God sent this boy so we could give him a loving home."

"No. God has a different plan for the boy. Think about our work schedules. You're gone all day Saturday and three nights a week. I don't get here until five. This house would be empty when he comes home from school. They'd never agree to place him with us."

"We could adjust our work schedules to do whatever it takes."

"No, we can't. We're not suited. We've made a different life for ourselves. We wouldn't have time alone together, and this child would cause stress between us. I've always believed I would do anything for you, Bobby, but I can't do this. I'm sorry."

Her rejection left him in shock. They sat without speaking until each got up from the table, Bobby and his dream crushed. He could not remember Nita ever refusing anything he'd asked. He spent the rest of the afternoon in the living room, with the television tuned to football games and his mind elsewhere.

Their silence continued. In the week that followed, Nita got up early to shower, dry her hair, and apply makeup. Bobby normally got up with her to share breakfast. But on these days without conversation, he stayed in bed until after she left for work, and did not come to bed at night until he knew she'd be asleep. On Monday he went out to eat alone, and on subsequent nights stayed late after taking his supper at the dealership. They did not attend their group's regular Saturday night party, and on Sunday morning Nita went to Mass by herself.

Bobby felt relieved to have some quiet time at home, to soul search and try to figure out why he'd been punishing both Nita and himself. During the week, he was less outgoing at work and his preoccupation resulted in poor sales numbers. New doubts about Nita and their marriage kept growing, and he'd begun to doubt himself. She had shut down all her maternal instincts and he never noticed the change. Maybe such natural tendencies had been channeled into mothering her husband instead. Did she now see him as a child? Their relationship and roles must have shifted imperceptibly.

He remembered suggesting Nita shorten her hair to a wash and wear length so she could save an extra hour in the morning, an idea she laughed off. Her clothes and appearance had become more and more important, to look attractive for people at the office, her job now her highest priority. He knew men were attracted to Nita. Maybe someone at work had captured her heart, a man much more accomplished than a car salesman. He wished he'd paid closer attention.

When Nita got home from church, she came straight into the living room and knelt down beside his chair. Fighting tears, she took his hand and looked into his eyes, ready to break their week-long silence. He braced himself to hear a confession, a confirmation of his worst fears, a truth no longer suppressed.

"Bobby, I have never loved you more than I do right now, enough to give you up and set you free so you can have children. I've failed you. I know we were married in the Church, but annulments are easier now. I won't stand in your way." She began sobbing, telling him over and over she loved him.

At that moment nothing else mattered, or ever would. Nita had said the words he needed to hear, letting him feel what he needed to feel. They were back where they started, the only place they ever needed to be.

He reached down and took her into his arms. They cried together until he spoke.

"I love you, too, Babe. I've been wrong about all of this, and I am so sorry. I hope you can forgive me. You were right, this home would never be right for the boy. You are all I need. It shouldn't have taken me this long to figure it out."

They went to the bedroom and made urgent, passionate love, their tears now from joy.

Just before Thanksgiving, Bobby and Nita found an animal shelter and adopted a rescue dog, a loveable black lab. The weather stayed mild into December, and the children at the orphanage continued playing outside. The boy no longer stood at the fence, and Bobby never saw him again. He guessed Sister Alicia had been able to place the boy after all.

A hope he would forever make himself believe.

SENSE OF TIME

Chilled by the fading dusk, worried about her mind, Madeline sat motionless on her screened porch. Summer's first cool night had arrived with a Canadian air mass sweeping the Illinois prairie, blowing away mid-August heat and humidity and dropping temperatures. Bundled in a heavy sweater last worn in early spring, she sniffed backyard dew as a chorus of crickets greeted the sudden cold. A sky without moon or clouds revealed a panorama of distant stars, in a universe partially obscured by the yellow glow from Chicago, forty miles east.

Madeline had been losing track of time. The episodes started shortly after Easter, ten or fifteen minute blank intervals prolonging quiet moments or routine chores. She would look up at a clock or down at her watch, surprised to read a time much later than expected. Unable to recall any distraction or broken train of thought, she could not account for discrepancies between her inner clock and the ticking timepieces. She hoped the interruptions were a symptom of aging, a normal mental regression experienced by a widow living alone in her seventy-ninth year. If the clocks weren't speeding up, then her brain had to be slowing down.

The time gaps increased in frequency, while she read the newspaper, took a shower, tried to fall asleep, lay awake in the morning, or sat with her thoughts. Some external force was stealing time, leaving her with less, no clue as to why. A fast-forward sun raced over the house, turning morning to afternoon, lengthening time-lapse shadows and speeding weather change. The spells and her anxious reactions repeated in cycles, periods of quiet worry extended by more missing minutes.

Everyone knew aging made time pass more quickly. Facial lines in Madeline's mirror said time distortions were a normal progression, but she suspected Alzheimer's or dementia, or mini-strokes. Apprehension grew as she considered each self-diagnosis.

The back of the house faced north. Madeline sat on the love-seat, part of a set of matching tables and chairs, weatherproof cushions resting on frames of white plastic pipe. Her late husband Charles had always sat beside her, marital bliss communicated as much by silence as conversation. Now she watched cell towers in the distance, blinking red heartbeats, synchronized signals to warn away aircraft and maybe extraterrestrials. Visible for miles, the pulsing lights had become spiritual communications from her departed husband.

Fertile scents from black earth cornfields wafted through spring and summer. Building the porch around an existing concrete patio had been Charles' idea. He'd overcome Madeline's reservations and ordered a do-it-yourself kit from Sears. After buying the necessary tools, he spent nights and weekends studying printed directions and assembling the pieces. The constructed porch, his proud creation, won her approval, a permanent gift from Charles filled with remembrances of serene moments, a place where she could still feel his unseen presence.

The marriage had been his idea, too, as was the decision to build their dream house on a rural road way out in the country. It all started by accident, when they physically collided in a lunchtime crowd on Michigan Avenue, he a young junior executive and she a copy editor for the *Chicago Tribune*. They met for lunch the next day and every day after. She was attracted by his quiet strength, self-assurance, and traditional values. Her instincts told her he was the one. They married the year Kennedy was elected and had two daughters by the mid-sixties. Charles worked hard to give them a happy life, his climb up the corporate ladder steady. She never regretted leaving behind the city and her career.

Every morning for forty years, Charles walked a quarter mile to a small wooden shelter at the railroad crossing where he caught the commuter train coming east from Geneva. They needed only one family car, always a station wagon or mini-van. Once the girls were old enough, Charles loved driving them on vacations to every corner of America, with local day trips reserved for weekends at home. Adventures, he called them. Even now, train sounds brought feelings of security to a house built beyond the reach of advancing subdivisions, Charles still a passenger leaving and coming home to her.

Family memories from her mental library flashed thousands of images of the two girls, Jane born two years after Marcia. She saw them in the morning, waiting together out on the road for the school bus or in snapshots of young sisters becoming women. Madeline struggled to understand why the mental photographs were still so sharp. If she was losing her mind, how could she recall every detail of family history? How could she calculate checkbook balances in her head and remember everything needed at the grocery store without a list?

Charles, now gone three years, left her one night in his sleep, dying as quietly as he had lived. If he were still alive, he'd be insisting she see a doctor. Obediently, she was driving into Wheaton in the morning for her annual appointment. She'd given blood and urine to the lab a week ago. If nothing significant turned up in the report, she'd have to voluntarily describe her lost moments to the physician.

**

She remained calm in the waiting room, silently rehearsing a testimony of her symptoms, until the door opened and a nurse called her name. "Madeline Monahan?"

A woman in sneakers and bright scrubs took her back to a small room, then keyed and clicked her records onto the computer screen. She stepped on a scale and offered an arm for the recording of blood pressure, then was ushered to another room to wait for the Doctor. He burst in with happy greetings and moved quickly to examine vital signs and reflexes. Then he took a seat at a second computer and recited an account of all the secrets documented in her lab report.

"Everything looks good, Madeline. I see good weight control and cholesterol levels. No changes since last time. Are you keeping up with your exercise?"

"Yes. Gardening, hours of house and yard work, although I pay someone to cut the lawn. I go walking when the weather's good, and do volunteer work when it isn't. At home, when I'm not reading or watching Cubs baseball, I make quilts."

"Stay active. I'm looking at good levels of blood sugar, sodium and uric acid. Looks like you're sticking to a balanced diet and taking your vitamins. No evidence of arthritis or joint problems, no abnormalities reported from your recent colonoscopy and dermatology evaluations. Heart very healthy, whatever you're doing seems to be working. Do you have any new complaints or problems we should be looking at?"

Whether he'd discovered something in the lab work or was simply asking a routine question, Madeline knew the moment had come to tell everything.

"Doctor, I've developed a mental issue these past few months, spells that occur daily. I can best describe them as short durations of amnesia, chunks of time slipping away while I'm working on something or sitting around thinking, everything normal until I look at a clock."

"Any dizzy spells, headaches or memory loss?"

"No. My memory is fine. I can name every one of my teachers, first grade through college. The disconnections don't register in my sense of time, and I can't recall my missing thoughts."

"Have you had problems driving your car?"

"No. Good concentration, always at the speed limit, but sometimes a trip takes longer."

"We could run tests, but you have no physical indicators on your chart. I'm inclined to believe these lapses have more to do with your emotional state, a psychological reaction to living alone with little human contact."

"Are you suggesting depression? I'm happy with my life. I love every day."

"No. Depression is marked by constant sadness, sleep disorders, and weight change. Or fear, which speeds pulse rates and internal clocks. Your daily routine has no deadlines or urgencies. Human perception of time, calculated by the brain, is subjective and variable. All of us have a different awareness of how long events take."

"What should I do?"

"Consider counseling. A professional might find the source of the gaps."

"I'm sure I don't need counseling, Doctor."

"Okay, then we'll monitor everything. I want to see you again in six months, with complete lab work. They'll give you the order sheet out front. Until then, I want you to be more active. Involve yourself with volunteer work, trips to see the kids and grandkids.

Increase the exercise, maintain a good diet, and reduce the idle time at home, less quilting and passive meditation. If any new problem develops, don't wait for the appointment. Get in here right away. Meanwhile, keep a log of new episodes and their durations."

"No medications?"

"You're not on any right now. Let's not fix what isn't broken."

"Thank you, Doctor."

Driving home, Madeline wondered if she should have mentioned the dreams, of bare rooms with clock hands spinning wildly, of a long tunnel where daylight collided with darkness every few seconds, of sunlight changing to rain and back in successive instants.

And she never told the Doctor about waking in the middle of the night and correctly guessing the time within five minutes. Relief from passing the physical exam was cancelled by frustration over unanswered mental questions. Why did her inner clock work so well while she was asleep?

***

Madeline made a list of do's and don'ts. She needed to cut down on quilting, reading and television. Cubs day baseball games could be watched, but not the ones played at night. Still mad about the lights added to Wrigley Field, her boycott of night games presented no hardship. The list of new activities included volunteer work at church and the library, serving as a poll worker for elections, and putting her name in as an emergency substitute for a bridge club. She toyed with the idea of writing a family history. Three phone calls had to be made immediately, to each of her two daughters and another to her dear friend, Pete.

She punched in the easy call first, to eldest daughter Marcia in Pennsylvania. An hour ahead, it was nearly suppertime back east, and Madeline knew her firstborn would be home, a middle school principal still working regular hours until students returned for the new school year. No need to worry about Marcia. She had it all, a college professor husband, two teenage boys, and a beautiful home.

"Mom! It's great to hear your voice! How are you feeling?"

"Well enough to invite myself to visit you at Christmas. Got room for an old woman? I'm ready to book my flight to Philadelphia."

"What a great idea. Come a few days early so you can see the boys play in their basketball tournaments. I'll have almost two weeks off to spend with you."

"When can you and the family come out this way?"

"Spring vacation would be best. It's hard to find a window in the summer that fits all our schedules. The boys have basketball camp, and Donald may sign up to teach a course."

"Then let's try for the spring. I can plan some stuff, maybe a Chicago Bulls basketball game and some train rides into the city, educational field trips like we used to take with Daddy."

"Great. I'll send you the dates. We'll drive out and skip the airport hassle. Maybe you can get together with Jane for Thanksgiving."

"You must have read my mind. I'm calling her next."

Before hanging up, they caught up on family news, Marcia bragging about the recent achievements of her three men. Madeline never mentioned her time lapse issue.

The next call was more difficult, to San Francisco, a time zone two hours behind, where younger daughter Jane worked as a prosecutor for the state attorney. Jane was tougher than her older sister, more competitive and career-driven. Divorced and childless, she needed more of Madeline's advice but was less inclined to take it.

"Jane, this is your Mother. I apologize for calling you at your office. If you're busy, I can call back when you get home."

"Now is a good time, Mom. I'm sitting here at my desk, working to put a bad guy away. What's up? Is everything all right?"

"Yes. Don't be alarmed. I want to get together with you for Thanksgiving, your place or mine. If you come this way, feel free to bring a boyfriend. I won't have a problem."

"I don't have a boyfriend. I'd rather you fly here and let me host. Book your flights on Mondays and we'll have a full week together."

"It seems such a waste, a beautiful woman like you without a man. I worry."

"Don't. I like my freedom. I get together with a fun group of couples and singles almost every weekend. People you will enjoy meeting. But I appreciate your concern."

"You're married to that job. You work too hard and too many hours."

"Work is great. Maybe I should be concerned about your constant worrying."

"I love you and care about you. I don't see or talk to you enough."

"We'll fix that at Thanksgiving. I worry about you, too. Maybe we can reassure each other."

"Okay. San Francisco, here I come. I'll be in touch. Take care of yourself, Jane."

"I love you, Mom."

Madeline thought the call went better than expected. Jane lived her life depending only on herself, a career woman enjoying her independence. Despite gradual acceptance of Jane's untraditional choices, Madeline still didn't like her living alone, with no man to love her.

The last call was to Pete, a neighbor. He'd been a widower only eighteen months. For years, they had double-dated with Pete and Winnie on Saturday nights, bowling followed by sandwiches, beer, and card games at their houses. Mated for life to their departed soul mates, Madeline and Pete did their best to keep some memories alive. They played cards. Gin rummy their game, penny a point, with a constant running debt never settled by either party.

"Pete, this is Madeline. I'm sitting here looking at your marker for ninety-seven dollars. Pay up, or get your sorry ass over here tomorrow night and do something about it."

"You're a tough old broad. You never talked like this when Charles was alive."

"I never had to. Bring your own beer, and money, lots of it."

"You get no mercy. I'll own you before the night is out."

"You'll have to play a lot better, Pete. Or find another game."

"Okay. I'll be the man ringing your doorbell at eight sharp."

"Game on."

Madeline put the cell phone on charge, and went out to the porch to relax after a long day of constant tension. She felt encouraged by the trip to the doctor, and the phone calls to her daughters. She sat there reliving past vacations and daydreaming about the new ones planned for the holidays and spring. After ten minutes, she went into the kitchen to fix supper, except the stove clock said she'd been on the porch for half an hour.

***

Pete arrived on time, and she ushered him to the same kitchen table where card games once were contested by two husband-wife teams. Madeline set out beer glasses, two decks and a score pad. Sandwiches and snacks were for later. They poured the beer and made conversation after complimenting each other's appearance.

"Madeline, I've got some concerns about that above-ground earth tunnel a few miles from here. What do you know about the experiments going on over there?"

"I wish I could remember Charles' detailed explanations. It's an accelerator laboratory, four miles in circumference. Scientists did high energy collisions with protons. The feds pulled the money and shut down the operation last year."

"How long has it been there?"

"They built it in the late sixties, when my girls were still toddlers. They put a small herd of bison in the center. We used to take the kids. It's still open to the public, dawn to dusk."

"It was up and running when Winnie and I built our house. Did you ever worry nuclear particle research might be a danger to people like us who live so close by?"

"No. Safety was never in question, though someone started an urban legend, claiming the bison were put there to provide a live warning if something went wrong."

Pete sighed. "Guess we'll never know the long-term health issues. Everyone's still alive. Deal the cards. I'm ready to start a new winning streak."

Their hard-fought games never encouraged much banter, but on this night Pete seemed unusually quiet. He abandoned his usual gambling style and piled up points with cautious strategy and the luck of the draw. Madeline's keen short-term memory usually won a majority of the long hands, but Pete was hot, and he hung in there. They still annoyed each other when they made rummy, he announcing "cribbage" instead of "gin" and she giving him the bad news with a condescending "My boy … and you *are* my boy … "

Pete won decisively and knocked twenty-seven dollars off his marker. She retrieved food from the refrigerator, and praised his victory as she poured the second beers.

"What's got into you, Pete? I've never seen you concentrate so well."

"Funny you should mention. I've been worrying about my powers of concentration lately. I'm a little embarrassed to talk about it."

"Go ahead. You didn't have any problems tonight. What's going on?"

Even as she asked the question, a premonition forewarned Pete's answer.

"It happens when I'm alone, senior moments when small blocks of time disappear and I have no recall of where they went. Something hacks into my brain and shuts it down until I can reboot. I'll bet you never heard of such a thing."

"Yes," she said. "I have."

MALCOLM AND MOLLY

Malcolm was working the Timesaver kiosk on a busy Saturday, selling a plastic wristwatch to a self-advertised gangbanger who paid with a twenty dollar bill. The guy was a wiseass with attitude wearing his ball cap backwards and pants on the ground, boxer shorts showing above the beltline. Placing the bill in the cash drawer, Malcolm noticed "Molly 555-9729" written in blue ink to the left of Jackson's portrait. Slammed with customers, he never had time to think about the name and phone number.

The bill reappeared when he was counting out at the end of the night. He peeled a twenty off his money clip and swapped for it. Best guess, Molly, whoever she was, wrote the information herself, a woman advertising availability. But something told Malcolm this wasn't a hooker drumming up business, and the tough guy customer who passed the bill was not her pimp. Thinking the number on the currency had been written by someone needing help, he thumbed it into his cell phone, placing the call as he walked across the parking lot to his car.

A girl answered, "Hello."

"This is Malcolm. Let me speak to Molly."

"This is she."

"You don't know me. I sell Timesaver watches out at the Mall. A customer gave me a twenty dollar bill today with your name and phone number written on it."

"And now you're calling 'cause you think I'm a whore?"

"No, I phoned because that's what I *don't* think. Somebody's putting your phone number out there. I thought you'd want to know."

"It's probably my ex-boyfriend. He got mad when I broke up with him. I'd know if I saw the handwriting."

"You should take a look, then. I could meet you at noon tomorrow at the mall food court. If the writing is his, you can decide what you want to do about it."

"Okay. Sit at a table in the Cinnabon area. How will I know it's you?"

"I'll be wearing a Yankees baseball jersey with the name 'Jeter' on the back. I look like Spike Lee, only taller."

***

Malcolm had been doodling on the back of a paper placemat when someone from behind knocked his baseball cap to the floor. Scrambling to retrieve it, he looked up to see a beautiful girl. She was wearing one of those crisp, sensible dresses he'd seen women wear to church, one that could not hide her sweet curves.

"Are you Malcolm Jeter?"

"No. I'm Malcolm Banks."

"Then who is Jeter?"

He wanted to tell her about his ageless baby-faced idol, a lock for the Hall of Fame after twenty seasons and five world championships, still drug-free at age forty, his last Yankee Stadium at-bat a game-winning hit, a model of class and dignity, girlfriends private, black father, white mother, a man for all races. But he gave her the simple explanation instead.

"Jeter is my hero, a baseball player who retired last year."

"I'm Molly Wade," she said, taking the chair opposite. "I'm not wearing my name on the back of my dress."

He liked her humor. "Sorry. Let me show you the twenty."

She recognized the handwriting immediately, her brown-eyed expression changing to the sad look of a woman disrespected. "That's him," she said. "He writes my name that way."

"I'll ink it out. Let's hope this is the only bill with your name and number on it."

"He was always bossing me. He came down to my nail salon and made a scene in front of everybody I work with, made me look real bad at my job. That was the final straw."

"Why were you with him?"

"He was sweet and polite at first. Then he joined a gang and started getting angry."

"Your salon is here on the mall?"

"Yeah, but I'm off on Sundays, when business is slow. I'm assistant manager. I run the cash register and sell the products."

She described her work with pride. He sensed her confidence, a girl with a plan for her future, and the day she would never have to depend on anybody.

"Young black woman promoted to management. Congratulations. You're on your way."

"Someday I'll have my own nail salon." He'd guessed right about her ambition.

"I work at the kiosk near Penney's," he said. "An assistant covers my Sundays. Someday I'll be selling Rolexes or Mercedes."

"Young black man crashes white establishment. They're not gonna let you wear that Jeter shirt. At least you're not flashing a backwards hat, like my ex. You got any tats?"

"Just one, a 'J' above my heart."

"I'm guessing it's for Jeter."

Malcolm made a mental note to not wear the Jeter shirt in public any more. Now he had to reveal a dark secret from an empty place in his heart.

"No. It's for my brother, Jess. He was killed in a drive-by shooting a few years back."

She gasped, whispering, "I'm sorry."

"He was at a party standing in the wrong place. Raised me like a father. Mama never recovered. She hardly goes out any more, except to church. I live at home so I can take care of her."

Molly nodded. "I live at home, too, trying to protect my mom from too many boyfriends. When they're not making her cry, they're hittin' on me."

Malcolm cringed from too much information. He changed the subject.

"Let's talk about the nail salon. What strategy do you use to sell products?"

"Just be pleasant, listen, stay patient. Make the customer feel comfortable."

"There's more to it. They have to feel they know you to reach that comfort level. My company tests personality profiles to help us sell better. I can test your profile, if you'd like."

"No test can tell anything about me."

"You'd be surprised. Take my pen, and on the back of this placemat, sketch a tree, a house, and a car. Use as much or as little detail as you like. When you're done, I'll explain to you what it all means."

Malcolm watched her draw, a child bent over her work with a tightly clutched pen, a food court vision. He asked to leave the table so she wouldn't feel nervous or rushed.

"Let me buy you a Cinnabon, so I can get rid of this bad

twenty. It's got a big ink square."

"I don't want you buying me anything."

"Don't be silly. I'm getting myself one, it's just as easy to ask for two."

He returned with the sweets as she finished her sketches.

"Let's see what you came up with."

Molly covered her paper with her hands, and handed back the pen. "Not so fast. I need to see *your* drawings."

"Okay, if you'll take a Cinnabon."

He sketched quickly, though his interpretations were more detailed. He'd taken the exam before, and easily recreated his previous effort. Discreet glances kept watch on Molly enjoying her sweet roll, breaking it into pieces with her fingers and taking one small bite at a time. Malcolm handed her his completed paper and watched her eyes study his work.

"Not bad. Now tell me what all this says about you."

"We'll do yours first. Starting with your tree, you got a wide trunk and a circle of thick foliage above. That says you're single-minded, with clear goals and great powers of concentration. Your summer tree reveals personal warmth, and so does the smoke coming out of the chimney on your house. But your branches are obscured, secrets you keep locked inside, seldom revealed to people. That's a problem when you're trying to make a sale."

"I make lots of sales."

"You'd do better if you weren't so guarded. People want you to open up with them. Your house is just a square, with no windows or sidewalk to invite folks in."

"Are you sayin' I'm unfriendly?"

"Your drawings say you're assertive, a girl demanding respect. But I'm saying there's a reason why our companies make us wear nametags."

"So we won't seem like strangers?"

"So we can connect. Your car is pointing to the right, which indicates you're still not sure about the direction you're headed. Not much detail in any of the drawings, indicating you don't get distracted by little things. You're able to focus."

"Now let's do your drawings."

"My tree is a winter tree with all bare branches, fork after fork branching farther and farther out. On the plus side, nothing is obscured, a tree that's all about honesty and trust. But too many branches mean I think too much and sometimes lose sight of the objective."

"You got a lot of detail on the house and car, too."

"My windows and sidewalk are open and welcoming, inviting trust. And the house, tree, and car are integrated in a single drawing, lined up on ground level, showing stability. My car points left, meaning I know where I'm going and how to get there."

"That's what worries me. This could be a game to win my trust."

"You should trust me. I want to date you."

"You're not worried my ex-boyfriend might kick your ass?"

"No. Not if you're done with him."

"I think I should wait. I just got rid of one boyfriend. I don't need another one. This doctor lady on the radio says you should wait one whole year after a breakup before movin' on to the next person."

"That advice is only for divorces and broken engagements."

"I need time to think. You seem nice enough, but I just met you. I like my life right now, free and uncomplicated."

"Does that mean 'no sale'?"

"I didn't say no. I'm just saying I'll wait to decide another day."

"When?"

"Sundays are bad around my house. After church, I never

know what condition my Mama will be in, or who might show up to yell at her. Wait for me here at this table the next three Sundays, between noon and one. If I miss all three, you'll know I decided not to date you. That's the best I can do. And never put 'Golly' in front of my name."

"Sounds like you're no fan of Little Richard."

"Nothing gets past you."

"I'll be here waiting. Hope you don't need all three Sundays."

"I might. I have to go now."

He stood up when she did, and watched her walk toward the mall exit.

***

Malcolm put on his best shirt and slacks and got to the food court early on the following Sunday. He waited well past one, but Molly never showed. She did not appear on the second Sunday, either. He braced himself for another no-show on the third Sunday, one that would close the book, leaving him rejected. It would be tough if he had to give up on her.

As the hour passed, he distracted himself by watching people and guessing the titles and words of songs played on the mall's piped-in music. What a fool he was, courting an empty chair in the food court. Food courting or fool courting, he'd struck out. But he knew he'd do it all over again. Molly was special, an intelligent, pretty girl who could change a guy, make him want to settle down. He knew lots of girls, but this one mattered, for reasons he had not yet figured out. She made him wish he'd already become a Mercedes salesman.

At ten after one, Malcolm sighed and pushed back his chair, finally giving up. He turned in time to see Molly appear from nowhere, smiling and walking slowly toward him.

"Hi, Malcolm."

"I didn't think you were coming. I waited here all three Sundays."

"I know. I came out here each week and spied on you to make sure."

"Does that mean you're gonna go out with me?"

"It means something better. I've decided to trust you."

BIKING ON
THE BEACH

In all seasons and nearly all weather, I bicycle a stretch of Florida beach on a sleek black beach cruiser. A sturdy no-frills machine, it has thick tires but no fenders, gears or hand brakes. At a different hour each day, low tide exposes hard-packed sand perfect for riding. Newspaper tide tables tell me when I can go, breathe the salt air and explore the continent's edge.

Winter winds make pedaling difficult but reward the eye with angry clouds and seas, dark waves spitting foam on a beach swept by wisps of loose sand. Now, in summer, biking is easier on repetitive humid days with prevailing breezes providing a protective buffer against inland thunderstorms. The blue-green, super-heated ocean delivers dangerous surf from a hurricane churning hundreds of miles east of the Gulf Stream. Pelicans glide single file above the breakers while groups of shore birds gather near the water line, waiting for the tide to turn.

That happens at noon today, the last August Saturday before kids go back to school. In bathing trunks, ball cap and flip-flops, I apply sunblock, grab a water bottle, make my way to the access ramp. I walk the bike through soft sand, mount up and turn right, heading south as always. Multi-million dollar homes line the first mile, a nearly-deserted stretch abandoned to isolated surfers, fishermen, and long distance walkers. Back near the dune, two young lovers recline on a blanket, secure in their privacy. She does not resist when the young man slips a hand inside her bikini, unobserved except by me, a discreet witness zipping past on a bike. Ahead, near tidal pools, a beautiful dwarf woman hunts alone for shells, smiling as she places each found treasure in a clear plastic bag. She was here yesterday, too, harvesting the same area with her short quick steps. Beyond the breakers, paddle boarders stand tall, appearing to walk on water.

Reaching the commercial zone, I find concentrations of beach-goers massed near timeshares, hotels, condos, and parking lots, every human form exposed for public display. My eyes search the crowd, a voyeur hiding behind sunglasses. The bike's exhila-rating freedom allows a moving vantage point to look, admire, and lust but imposes loneliness on a journey without pause or conversation, only silent nods from oncoming walkers or bicy-clists. Surveying the sunbathers, taking visual snapshots, I keep one cautious eye on the sand ahead, vigilant for darting small children and the deep holes they love to dig.

Attractive women can be seen texting, but age disqualifies me from the young and semi-young. Inked with multiple tattoos, female millennials in their skimpy swimsuits leave little to the imagination with artwork meandering to intimate places. The painted bodies of their men sport permanent engravings advertis-ing strength on chests, arms and shoulders. Love is in the air. Couples hold hands, be they elderly, age-disparate, interracial, or same sex, each pairing a new normal in an inclusive society.

Two miles down the beach, high rise buildings mark the border of the next city and my turnaround point. Southerly breezes fa-cilitate pedaling on the return trip, but it's hotter with the wind at my back, requiring a brief stop for the water bottle. Pausing to view this strip, I see beach toys everywhere, tossed footballs, beanbags and Frisbees, balls bowled to targets, soccer balls, paddleballs, handballs, coaxed kites. Tents shield sun-sensitive spectators, sheltered in their chairs under colored canvas stretched between aluminum poles. Wave riders shriek with delight. Everyone else grips or studies a cell phone. Shrimp boats and pleasure craft dot the horizon while planes above tow banners advertising suntan lotion and beer.

In motion again, nearing the elite residential zone, what's this? A woman jumps out in front of my bike, her raised palms signaling me to stop. Her gray-white hair defies advanced age while her black bikini flaunts a younger woman's figure. Pushed-back sunglasses reveal intense blue eyes and smiling character lines as she grabs the handlebars and straddles my front tire.

"My name is Kate. Who might you be?"

"I'm Steve. Do I know you?"

"You should. You've been ogling me all summer, twice a day coming and going. I'm hurt you never stopped to talk."

"Did I give a wrong impression?"

"Hell, no. I want you to look. That's why I starve myself and spend money on yoga classes and the gym. My underwear at home hides more than this bathing suit."

"Money well spent. You look great, Kate."

"You're not so bad yourself with your shirt off. I don't know who you're searching for, but I've been sitting right here in my chair every day, hiding in plain sight. I'm assuming you're single, prefer women, and live somewhere up the beach."

"Three correct assumptions. Am I young enough for you?"

"Let's find out. Meet me tonight at Danny's for a drink, say around eight, and we'll continue this conversation. Should I save a seat for you at the bar, Steve?"

"Please. I'll be there."

Letting go of the bike, she says, "Okay. I'll look for you."

Riding home, I'm stunned to have found someone, or has she found me? Both of us hiders, deciding to come out, come out, whoever we are, hoping to win the same game. Kate's aggressive but witty and sexy. I don't remember noticing her on previous expeditions. She certainly has my attention now.

If we click, I've got an extra beach cruiser for her. Maybe we'll bike together.

THE DOOMSAYER

Flashing lights from city police and county sheriff patrol cars reduced traffic to a crawl as curious drivers rubber-necked looks at the handcuffed man on the sidewalk. The scene straddled the county line, with officers from two jurisdictions trying to decide who would arrest the detainee, a short, bare-chested, homeless-looking troll of a man. Endless days in the sun had bronzed his skin and bleached his shoulder-length hair and full beard. Locals knew him as the man who yelled at condos.

As my car inched past, I could see his cuffed profile positioned on the county side of the green city limit sign, giving authority for the collar to the deputy sheriff calling it in on his radio. Until today, the suspect had always been able to move a few feet north or south if police showed up. Two law enforcement agencies had now come for him in a synchronized operation.

For almost a year, standing on his spot in the same ragged cutoff shorts and dusty high top shoes, this shaggy sidewalk evangelist angrily ranted at southbound cars, buildings and their inhabitants, and to anyone close enough to hear him predicting the world's imminent end. A Doomsayer, obsessed with telling us time had run out, confirming our death sentence with non-stop declarations and warnings:

"No one is listening. None of you have any idea."

"The end is near. Get ready."

"I told you, God always has the last word."

"None of this had to happen. Now it's too late."

"We've poisoned this earth and it's time to pay."

"Everyone forgets, the Lord is watching."

"We should have seen this coming."

"Make your peace, pray for your souls."

"The world will end on television."

His hoarse voice alternately croaking and barking, the Doom-sayer's public outcries were punctuated by raised arms, gestures, and body language signaling anger and hostility. He shouted at clouds, shook his fist at planes towing advertising banners over the ocean, and snarled at people yelling taunts from passing cars. Teens threw quarters and beer cans at him.

"Get a job old man!"

"You're a nut case."

"We're coming back to kick your ass."

"Find a new drug."

"God doesn't exist."

The object of their ridicule answered each jeer, assuring all non-believers they would burn in hell, yelling back f-bomb ob-scenities without taking the Lord's name. The Doomsayer had an uncanny ability to make eye contact with every driver zooming past at forty miles per hour, as if probing the soul of each motor-ist crossing his field of vision. His relentless fury invited conflict. Someone had taken offense, a car passenger or a pedestrian, maybe a dog walker or a parent with scared children, agitated enough to phone a complaint to the police. Or maybe the cops were serving a warrant for a transgression committed away from his roadside pulpit.

I watched him roaring at his uniformed captors, damning them for tormenting him, screaming at bystanders to stop this police brutality. But Doomsayer's outlaw appearance and hoarse protests reinforced the case against him. His scary translucent blue eyes locked on mine as my vehicle inched past, the deputy palming his head to guide him into the back seat of the squad car. His objections silenced, he recognized me, his surprised expression reflecting the shock of a man betrayed.

Yes, my face was familiar because I knew him, well enough to classify myself a follower. I'd been studying him since the previous summer, after first spotting the man on a drive home from Publix. Closed windows in my air-conditioned car muffled his non-stop monologue but aroused a curiosity to learn what he was saying. From that day forward I would look for him, at first in my car and later walking or riding a bicycle through his territory on trips that became more frequent, groceries stuffed in a backpack and a handlebar basket. I would slow as I passed him, straining to hear his words, brief rasping sound bites that faded as I kept moving to avoid attracting his attention. Occasionally he'd receive a friendly honk and wave at a car he knew.

If the man's anger targeted condo inhabitants, that wrath could have applied to me, an owner of a modest unit just down the road, where I hoarded a private view of the endless blue ocean. My guilt was mitigated by my low rise building, rejected by cliff dwellers living in high rise structures blocking the sun and casting shadows on the beach.

I felt rewarded whenever I encountered Doomsayer, whether he was at his post guarding his domain or pacing a three block stretch of sidewalk. Late mornings and afternoons he could be seen talking and walking, shouting and muttering, standing at his ministry gesturing to the heavens. On hot days, he favored sitting with his arms cradling his knees, a pack of cigarettes and a lighter on the pavement beside him, sometimes a lit one dangling from his fingers between puffs. For relief, he'd hike to the strip mall and supermarket, where I once heard his graveled voice reciting a fast-food breakfast menu as if it were a poem, ignored by individuals pushing their shopping carts past him, people pretending he wasn't there.

Summer heat dissipated in October, and Doomsayer, still in cutoff shorts and construction boots, became less visible as winter approached. By December, he'd acknowledged the cooler temperatures by wearing, every single day, a brown Jack Daniels tee shirt commemorating a motorcycle event from 2006. That month, I saw him walking a side street away from the highway, heading into a cul-de-sac of upscale residences. I wanted to believe the man had a home after all, with one or more family members to look after him, waiting to make his lunch. I started looking down this street whenever he was absent from the highway, and spotted him coming or going more than once, moving with the fluid athletic grace of a halfback or a shortstop, quietly muttering to himself.

"The Lord sent the wildfires to Florida."

"He gave us hell on earth."

"We did it to ourselves."

"God always wins."

Researching this muttering delirium, I learned periodic low utterances were a sign of motor restlessness in individuals who felt persecuted. Such people performed strict rituals as a defense, never letting their guard down in seeking safety and security, despite exhibiting disorganized, delusional behavior. Hyperactive, constantly in motion, and talking non-stop through hallucinations, anti-social mutterers created compulsive coping mechanisms to deal with anger issues and daily irritations. I did not know if all these characteristics applied to Doomsayer but many of the tendencies seemed to fit. He was either deranged or a disciple, possessed by the devil or a recruiter for God, asking no offerings. I would have given him water, money and cigarettes if such tributes could have been made without compromising my anonymity.

As Easter neared, I began seeing Doomsayer bent over the sidewalk sketching or writing. A bicycle expedition revealed he'd been leaving messages and short passages of scripture in white chalk. The upper case letters stretched for more than three blocks in varying degrees of legibility, mostly quotations from the Bible, with references to Moses and the pharaohs. Warnings inserted at regular intervals protested cops and their power to murder people, connecting God's revelations to police unlawfully firing their weapons. Spring rains washed everything away overnight but our prophet would be back the next morning, hunched over his work. I wondered where he got his abundant supply of chalk, and whether such inscriptions on the public sidewalk might be illegal.

When I described these writings to a friend, she said she knew someone who'd been married to the guy long ago. He'd once been a normal, beloved husband. One day something in him snapped, the wife divorced him, and he'd behaved this way ever since.

Celebrating the summer solstice, I drove to the strip mall and ordered soup at the Chinese fast food. Stepping next door to the Family Dollar for a box of crackers, I discovered Doomsayer standing with his cigarette purchase, preaching to the clerk. With no tattoos, he looked fit and healthy, despite his damaged voice. Surprisingly perfect teeth flashed beneath albino eyebrows and eyelashes. He was telling the kid at the counter the world's end would be televised. We'd all be able to watch our impending doom on every channel. I'd never been this close to the man, and hung on every word until he left.

The clerk shook his head and said "That guy's a crazy man," before directing me to the cracker aisle. It occupied a dimly lit dead end in a distant corner of the store.

Pondering the selections and reading the calorie counts, I was unaware of the person who had quietly approached and now stood beside me. I turned to look into the penetrating eyes of Doom-sayer, who had returned to the store to ask me a question. Cornered and startled, his face inches from mine, I tried not to show fear.

"You've been watching me. Why?"

"I see you whenever I come up here."

"You're not following me?"

"No. I'm just shopping."

"But you've been listening."

"Yes," I said.

"What do you hear?"

"Lots of things."

"Then you know the world is going to end, that we'll see it on television."

"I've heard you say that."

"Do you believe it?" he asked.

"I don't know. How soon will it happen?"

"Soon. We must prepare."

"Okay. Thanks. I'll be watching."

"Good."

He turned on his heel and left me to compose myself and pay for my purchase. The next time I saw him he was under arrest and handcuffed in the sheriff's patrol car. Whenever we see the police take someone away, we assume that person has done something wrong. Doomsayer looked guilty. Maybe the authorities had to deal with him as a terrorist, investigating the man to find out what made him so certain the world was going to end.

It's been a year now without seeing the Doomsayer, and I don't know if he was incarcerated, committed, or if he's passed on.

I still look.

ACCIDENTAL
DEATHS

In the basement beneath the ancient school building, Joseph finished his test and listened to faint sounds penetrating the quiet of his sixth grade classroom. A ticking wall clock, humming fluorescent lights, suppressed coughs, shuffled papers, and a dropped pencil echoed off the tile floor. Just below the ceiling, small ground level windows muffled outdoor noise and filtered winter afternoon light. Melting snow promised an early spring, and Joseph counted the days to baseball season as he studied the sweet profile of his secret crush, Maureen, sitting several seats away. He had never admitted this affection to anyone, content to hold dreams of someday winning her heart.

A soft knock broke the silence. Mrs. Wolfe stepped into the hall to speak to someone and returned to Joseph's desk, whispering instructions to fetch his wool cap from the coat hook and follow her outside. The Principal, Miss Atkinson, waited with a smaller kid and two mothers. Joseph's had been summoned because her son stood accused. The younger boy claimed to have been pushed into a goldfish pond by an older boy wearing a red stocking cap with white tassel, a hat now entered as evidence against its owner. The victim had arrived home for lunch in dripping wet clothes and was now making positive identification. When the kid finished his story, the court of inquiry turned to the defendant, anticipating his confession.

No one spoke, until Joseph's mother asked, "Did you push this boy into the pond?"

"No."

She turned to Miss Atkinson and calmly entered a not guilty plea. "He didn't do it."

"How can you be sure, Mrs. Rafferty?"

"Joseph is a handful, but he never lies. May I go now?"

Facing cross-examination, the plaintiff hung his head and began crying, case dismissed. Everyone climbed the stairs as Mrs. Wolfe ushered the acquitted defendant back inside. He felt the stares of his classmates as he sat down. Minutes later, he was passed a note.

It said, "Joseph, I believe you. Maureen."

She had heard everything from her seat near the door. Validated by her declaration, he carefully re-folded the paper, her handwritten words a treasure to be kept.

Later, the Principal called Joseph's mother to apologize. The smaller boy had followed Joseph as he ran a short cut behind some corner houses on his way home to lunch, hurdling flower beds and leaping a rectangular goldfish pond. His pursuer failed to jump the pond and fell in, inventing an alibi to explain his soaked clothing.

Joseph's mother recounted the boy's revised story when her son got home. "I'm sorry you were wrongly accused. That's why you must always tell the truth, so no one will ever doubt you."

Maureen believed him. But he had never told anyone the truth about his feelings for her. He'd fallen that first day when she entered class newly rezoned from another school. Irish blue eyes, pale white skin, dark curly hair, and a soft voice, her serene demeanor expressing an easy smile or a hint of one.

At age twelve, the reasons for his attraction to her still unknown, he only knew his crush on Maureen Rae made him feel good. She was both class beauty and class brain. To be worthy, he became a model student to gain her respect, in marked contrast from his previous academic indifference.

Physical education classes offered opportunities to be her champion, surviving ten throws as the last kid standing in dodgeball or rescuing her in a tag game of capture, running to set her free by taking her hand and racing back to the safety zone.

Joseph missed Maureen on weekends, barely noticing the warming weather. Sweet spring days soon yielded to dreaded summer. On the last school day, he smiled goodbye but did not approach her. His Little League baseball games drew large crowds and he searched the grandstand for his dark-haired beauty but never saw her. Pretending she was watching helped him play better. As summer wore on, Joseph sometimes bicycled to her part of town, hoping to catch a glimpse of her while passing her house.

Seventh grade, long anticipated, arrived without her. A redrawn district had transferred Maureen back to her former school. Saddened, bored, with no love interest or hope, Joseph became a discipline problem, firmly dealt with by Mrs. Morris, a huge deep-voiced woman with zero tolerance for distracted students. Her sunny classroom, located on a south corner of the second floor, always felt too bright and hot after a year in the cool basement. She punished misbehavior by dropping a dictionary on the offender's desk and flipping it open.

"Print the entire page by hand and have it on my desk in the morning or I call your mother."

Her finger pointed to the even-numbered page on the left, but Joseph, in a tiny act of rebellion, always printed the odd-numbered page on the right, an easier task for a right-hander.

The aged school became a prison as long weeks dragged one season into the next. When warm days returned, huge open windows let in fresh air and the occasional bird, wasp, or dragonfly. Voices from the grassless playground outside distracted, laughter taunting those trapped inside. Joseph's misconduct, punished by solitary confinements in the coat room, earned a sentence of permanent probation until summer's full pardon.

In the fall, bad luck continued, separating Maureen and Joseph in two eighth grade sections taught in the high school, students passing between adjacent classrooms twice a day. She had grown more beautiful during their year apart, and he experienced the pleasure-pain of seeing her for brief seconds each morning and afternoon, struggling to make eye contact as their single file lines trudged in opposite directions between the doorways.

Ninth grade was another lost year, with no common classes and only brief observations of Maureen sitting with her girlfriends in the cafeteria. Joseph suffered without speaking to her, his unyielding shyness discouraging any thought to try.

That winter, a tragic accident on a rural two-lane took the life of a boy in the senior class. His car slid off the road in a snowstorm, and he was struck and killed by another car as he walked to get help. On a spring day months later, students gathered on the school's front lawn for a tree-planting ceremony as a pastor led them in prayer.

Joseph did not notice Maureen standing beside him until she asked a question.

"Did you know him?"

"No," he answered. "I'd see him between classes but we never spoke."

"It doesn't seem possible, Joseph. We used to see him walking the halls and now he's a tree in front of the school."

"I'll still think of him as a person. I've never known anyone who died."

"I have," she said. "When I was seven, my baby brother strangled to death in his crib."

He mumbled, "I'm sorry, Maureen."

"My brother's in heaven now. It was an accident, no one's fault." She reassured Joseph by touching his hand before she walked away.

Summer brought the death of someone Joseph knew. A town policeman who lived a few doors away shot and killed his wife. He was loading his gun, getting ready for his shift, when she walked into the bedroom and startled him. He turned and the gun went off, sending a bullet through her heart. People questioned how a man trained in handling guns could make such a mistake. The shooting death was ruled accidental.

Joseph finally shared a class with Maureen in tenth grade, an advanced biology course that included sex education. Boys sat on one side of the room, girls on the other, asking no questions while a monotone teacher explained human reproduction. Joseph watched her take meticulous notes, a "straight A" student certain to become class valedictorian.

Everything ended abruptly in eleventh grade, just after Easter break. Joseph's locker partner told him the news. Maureen had become pregnant. Her innocence taken at age sixteen, she had left school and no one would be seeing her again. Joseph's innocence had died too, an indirect casualty of the same accidental conception. The father-to-be, David Drake, was a nineteen year-old who lived on a farm and owned a car. Joseph could not imagine Maureen sneaking around with him or letting him have his way. Drake must have forced himself on her.

The distance to the high school baseball field was six long blocks. Joseph, varsity second baseman, endured practice with a heavy heart, his grieving intensified on the long trek back with metal spikes dragging on the pavement. Maureen's departure took away something good, leaving emptiness and anger in its place. As players pulled off their uniforms in the locker room, Richie Hagen called out Maureen's name and made animated, vulgar references to the act causing her pregnancy. Hagen, senior catcher, was a full-grown specimen with a thick mat of chest hair. Exploding with rage, Joseph rushed over and pushed him into his locker, slamming the metal door against his head. A boy attacking a man, the element of surprise allowed him to gain the upper hand with Hagen's arms still stuck in his uniform sleeves. Teammates pulled them apart.

"Are you crazy?" Hagen shouted.

"Watch your mouth!" Joseph yelled, struggling against those holding him back.

The story of the fight circulated quickly, a rare conflict where a little guy jumped a big guy. Opinions differed over whether Joseph was someone not to be trifled with or an unstable powder keg, ready to blow at the slightest provocation. Either way, his wary peers steered clear, and no one ever snapped a towel at him again. Hagen sought him out and apologized man-to-man, and Joseph's tough guy reputation stuck, falsely created by a single reckless moment defending the honor of Maureen Rae.

He lost interest in baseball, quitting before his senior season, and asked a girl to the prom. At graduation, Joseph could not stop thinking about the new mother who should have been there. His last name followed hers in the alphabet, Rafferty after Rae, and she would have been sitting next to him. He imagined her receiving her diploma just before he got his, then holding her close in a warm celebration hug after they left the stage. But the dream vanished, and he graduated without her.

Joseph enrolled in a commuter college and four years went by in a blur, hours and days crowded by study and a part-time job with a grocery chain. He dated a few girls, one steadily, but she went abroad for a semester and met a man in Italy. The cop who shot his wife remarried and was promoted to plainclothes detective. A law school accepted Joseph's application but he decided to wait, work another year at a full-time job and bank the money for tuition. He lost track of Maureen and never knew what became of her.

The law school decision required telling his boss at the grocery store not to hold his job, to schedule him only as a substitute so he could go into the city and search for a permanent position. They loaned him out to other stores one or two days a week, wherever he was needed to man a cash register, trim produce, or stock shelves. Trained to perform any assignment, he spent the mindless hours of work thinking and planning his future.

Just before Thanksgiving, assigned to another store in another town, Joseph punched out and walked two blocks to lunch in a cafeteria. He finished his meal and was stacking dishes on his tray when he looked up and saw Maureen Rae, sitting in a corner of the dining room with three small children. His first impulse was to bolt, leave before she spotted him, but he overcame his fear and approached her table. She recognized him immediately, calling out his name in happy surprise and jumping up to give him a tight hug.

"Joseph! It's been years!"

He held her embrace before letting go and replying, "It's great to see you, Maureen."

She asked about his life, and he summarized it in a few sentences. Now twenty-two, she still looked sixteen, with no visible sign of weariness or fatigue from birthing and mothering three young kids. She introduced two boys, ages five and three, and a little girl in a high chair who would soon be two. Her well-behaved children smiled at him as they ate their food without hurry.

"David's doing really well. He's a contractor and has three crews building houses. He built one for us, and we moved in last week. We're looking forward to Christmas in our new home."

Maureen had become a wonderful wife and mother. She could have excelled at any career she wanted, but glowed happiness in the life she had chosen. Joseph's childhood affection and adolescent love for her had not been misplaced.

"Your children are beautiful."

"*Life* is beautiful," she said.

Her quiet certainty resolved nagging questions and lifted the weight of a long-suffered loss. Dreams died with or without people, all accidental deaths. Survivors moved on. He knew he'd never see Maureen again, and now it no longer mattered. Their chance meeting had given him everything he would ever need.

Joseph embraced her one last time and wished her well, grateful for her gift of closure.

FRACK, FRACKING, FRACKED

Tom Carter's forbears settled a small valley in northern Pennsylvania, clearing the bottom land and leaving the steep upland slopes pristine. For two centuries, generations of Carters stood their ground, farming the acres through good years and bad, his father's father building the current house and the dirt road connecting it to the highway. Two sons, grown and gone to distant cities, became university professors with wives and children. Left without their help, Tom took his sons' advice and leased the fields to contract farmers. A lean and craggy-faced Marlboro Man, he spent idle days walking the wooded hill, a good vantage point to view the annual cycle of tilled soil, nurtured crops, and mechanized harvests. His wife Edie, small and frail, kept to their home down below, tending goats, chickens, and cats. Evenings, Tom would read from a home library while Edie quilted, both of them content to quietly grow old together.

Natural wonders still surprised Tom on his daily walks. Wildlife emerged from hiding, birds called, silent deer foraged, black bears and mountain lions left tracks. Each change of season unveiled new artwork on freshly painted landscapes. Shafts of summer sunlight dropped through the trees, branches dripping morning dew as noisy streams gurgled from higher elevations.

Dense green foliage morphed into brilliant autumn colors, viewed and photographed by visitors from New York and Philadelphia on mid-October weekends. Winter repainted nature's canvas a final time, before its white still life melted into spring's renewal.

One summer, all of it changed. Walking a higher elevation, Tom felt the mountain shake beneath his feet as birds took flight from a shattered peace. Down at the house, faint tremors rattled windows and frightened the animals. Edie was frantic by the time her husband returned from his hike.

"What is going on, Tom? The china cabinet has been shaking and the cats are hiding. Are we having an earthquake?"

"No. I saw flatbed trucks on the road carrying heavy machinery, and dust clouds have been drifting over the ridge. I'm guessing they're clearcutting forest on the other side."

"Is it strip-mining?"

"Could be. I'll find out what's making all the noise, I promise."

Despite his reassurance, Edie continued to fret. Their home had never been rattled like this, not even during severe thunderstorms. Up on the highway, more flatbeds brought loads of pipe and pieces of infrastructure, followed by cement mixers and an endless parade of tankers. Tom called a town official and learned the trucks carried water and toxic chemicals. Injected deep into the earth under intense pressure, the liquids hydraulically fractured underground shale to extract natural gas.

Weeks later, after contractors trucked away the corn crop, Edie, canary in the mine, noticed an odd taste in the water, with an odor becoming stronger each day. On a hunch, Tom turned on the faucet and lit a match, igniting a steady flame, startling both of them. Gas had contaminated their well, but how? They began buying bottled water for drinking. Tom contacted a county agent to come out and do tests.

"It's gas, all right. Your water is too toxic for drinking, bathing, or doing your laundry. Don't quote me, but it's probably seepage from the gas drilling down the road. They encase the well in concrete but the fracking pressure causes cracks and the bad stuff leaks out."

"How long until we're able to use the well again?"

"You'll be shut down until they stop drilling, and maybe for some time after that."

After the county man left, Edie broke down in tears. Tom did his best to comfort her, holding her tight until she stopped sobbing. She'd been complaining about a skin rash. Now they knew why the agent said no bathing. Their water, life-sustaining and taken for granted, had been poisoned, leaving the future uncertain.

"I don't want you worrying," he said. "We'll figure out a way to deal with this."

"What will we do for water?"

"I'll go get a temporary supply and bring it back in the truck."

"Can the grandchildren still come for a visit this summer?"

"No. Not until this problem is resolved."

Tom drove his pickup into town and bought a five hundred gallon plastic tank at the farm supply store. They sent him around back for the water, where three other customers had backed in, paying a small fee to fill their tanks. When he got home, he parked the setup near the kitchen door so Edie could fill jugs for drinking and cooking. They rigged some old curtains for outdoor bathing, and began taking their laundry to the nearest laundromat ten miles away.

Incessant water trucks and chemical tankers intensified the noise and dust. Twenty-four seven, fracking never ceased. Hoping for a closer look, Tom took a ride down the highway to the site, where a man in a hard hat greeted him at the gate.

"I live a few miles up the road. I've been curious about what you're doing down here."

"We're producing clean energy. Step inside and I'll give you a tour."

Tom put on a visitor's hard hat. His guide explained the operation and bragged about how it contributed millions of dollars to every level of government. A steel straw sucked from an underground ocean, huge tanks capturing natural gas and the backflow from injected chemicals. A pipe vented a flaming plume of flammable vapors, making the air reek of methane and money

Tom thanked him for his time, never mentioning the problems with his well water or his wife's distress. With so few people living in the region, he could see why county and state governments had granted the permits. America needed energy, corporations and governments needed cash.

Edie's health worsened, probably from the gas fumes in the air, and she suffered headaches, dizziness, and breathing difficulties. Tom drove her down to Scranton to see a doctor. He had already treated numerous fracking exposure cases, not only to airborne methane but also to chemicals dumped on the ground or in retention ponds. Glycol, ethane, benzene, carbon disulfide, hydrochloric acid, all the volatile toxins used to frack were known carcinogens. The physician prescribed an ointment for her rash and advised her to stay indoors with windows closed. As long as they remained on the farm, Tom knew Edie would not get better.

Returning home, they found sickly cats losing hair, and a favorite goat dead. Tom buried the animal, Edie crying until she ran out of tears.

"What are we going to do?" she asked.

"I don't know. We may have to leave and go stay with my brother."

"But Tom, our home is here. We can't live our lives as someone's guests. And we wouldn't be able to take the cats and goats."

"Let's deal with it one day at a time. There has to be an answer."

Days later, hiking in the upland forest, Tom discovered dead rabbits, birds and frogs. Near a stream, gas bubbled and fizzled from the ground. Again, his lighted match ignited a flame. Walking back down the slope, he got a nosebleed.

By now, other people were reporting similar problems, and local media began closely covering the developing story. Public complaints were filed, but the company denied responsibility, claiming toxic chemicals blasted eight thousand feet below ground had no impact on the water table, insisting no methane had escaped from the well casings. Tom and Edie attended a public meeting in town, where a state agent met with a gathering of property owners. They raised many questions but the entire problem was explained in a single answer:

"All underground water is connected. Fracking probably caused the contamination, but this drilling was exempted from the 2005 Clean Water Act. Your complaint hearings will take years and require expensive lawyers, with no guarantee you'll ever be able to prove corporate liability or win any compensation. It's not fair, but those are the facts."

Edie shook with anger on the drive home.

"Tom, how can they destroy everything we have, everything we've worked for?"

"I'm just as confused as you are. The system seems to be working against us."

"Don't we have rights?"

"We do, but we're just little people."

One of Tom's sons put him in touch with a scientist who

phoned an explanation: contaminated fracking chemicals could not be naturally filtered underground. Studies yielded the same conclusions in region after region. The poisoning was irreversible. The fields could no longer be farmed. The well water could cause the house to blow up if they lit a match or used the fireplace when the weather got colder.

Tom went back into town to see a real estate agent, to find out if the land could be sold with full disclosure about the contaminated well.

"Sorry, Tom, but I've been giving the bad news to every property owner in the fracking zone: Your lands cannot be sold at any price. There are no buyers."

"So what do I do, just walk away?"

"You could, if you own the land free and clear."

"That still leaves me on the hook for the property taxes." He suddenly had a vision of his land being sold by the county in a sheriff's auction.

When Tom got home, he sat Edie down and carefully explained why they had to leave.

"We can't stay here. We'll pack what we can in the camper, and drive to Iowa to live on my brother's farm. When we see how much space he has, I'll come back here for another load."

"What about our pets?"

"We'll find a farm to take the goats and the chickens, and place the cats in an animal shelter. They will all die if they stay here."

In a daze, Edie listened without responding. Increasingly withdrawn, she'd finally shut down. It took a week to pack and seal the house. Deciding what to take or leave was as painful as giving up the animals. A man from the other side of the county brought a livestock trailer to haul the goats and the chickens. Tom drove the emaciated cats to the shelter. They cried all the way, as if sensing no one would adopt them.

The couple left in the middle of the night so they could reach their destination by sunset the next day. Tom stopped the camper on the highway, headlights shut off and the motor running. He retrieved his high power .30-06 rifle from the back and sighted its telescope on the well-lit fracking structure three hundred yards away. His target was the eight inch chemical backflow pipe the hardhat had shown him. The last Carter to leave the land would not go quietly.

He waited for his heart and breathing to settle before squeezing the trigger. The bullet ignited a small flame in the pipe, fire traveling to the condensate tanks and the gas well. The explosion turned the night sky orange, lighting the entire county.

Tom got back in the camper and headed for Iowa, the receding glow of the fire shining on his rear view mirror. He had no regrets about what he had done, and no worries about getting caught.

Neither of them spoke for an hour, until Tom whispered, "I love you, Edie."

CRIMINOLOGY

"Not failure, but low aim is crime."

Professor Ryan wrote the quote on the blackboard as his class filed into the windowless room and took their seats. His students carried no books or writing materials, only a readiness to answer questions and give their opinions in a rapid-fire group discussion. Each answer would generate new questions from an instructor probing human behavior and motives.

Ryan used the first twenty minutes to continue the previous week's inquiry, a debate over whether criminal acts were the result of rational or irrational choices. The class concluded crimes were impulsive or calculated, sometimes both. Accepting their verdict, the professor closed the topic and turned to the quote on the blackboard. Taking a piece of chalk, he added the attribution, "from a poem by James Russell Lowell, 1868."

"What is Lowell trying to say here?"

Hands went up, offering interpretations. "Set high goals." "Don't fear failure."

"Challenge yourself."

"Not trying is worse than failing."

"To summarize, you say setting easy goals is a crime, so is not trying, and it's wrong to be afraid to fail. *Fear,* our reaction to anxiety or danger. Can *fear* be a crime?"

The question drew a long silence as his students searched for an answer. Fear was an emotion everyone felt but no one wanted to admit or talk about.

Finally, Walter offered an example, describing the classic dilemma of a witness. "A person could see someone do something bad and be too afraid to stop it or report it."

"Why would anyone be afraid to report a crime? Aaron?"

"People are scared to get involved. And no one wants to be a snitch. They might end up as the next victim."

"Those committing the crimes, what do *they* fear? Darnell?"

"They're afraid of being nobodies and never getting any-where."

"You're saying poverty contributes to criminal behavior, something we talked about last month. Jerome, do the perpetrators fear anything else?"

"As Darnell said, they're afraid of being poor, of never finding a way out. But fear can be about losing respect, like in a gang, where a dude has to be cool to be accepted, and do the crime with everybody watching. I've seen it happen."

"It's called peer pressure. Jerome says showing fear means an absence of courage. Is he right?"

Robert disagreed. "No. People can be scared, but still do brave things. They're more afraid of what might happen if they don't step up. Superstars fear losing and make plays to win games. Fear helps you concentrate in tough situations."

"So fear can be a good thing, a motivator. Fear of death helps soldiers survive in war. That raises a whole new question. Is war a crime? Carlos?"

"For one side it is. In a war, we think anything the enemy does is a crime. But when guys on our side kill so they won't be killed, or kill civilians by mistake, we're okay with that."

"Last week, we agreed terror is crime. Do terrorists fear anything?"

Hands went up. Louis got the call. "The people they're trying to hurt. And they fear those who give them their orders. They pass that fear down to innocent people who don't know where or when the next act of terror is going down. That's the whole purpose."

"Are you saying terror makes people afraid to come out of their homes?"

"At first they are. Then they have to get on with their lives, go back to school or go to work to earn a living. Put food on the table."

"Once they've put fear in people's minds, why do terrorists keep killing? Isaac?"

"They don't like people who are different from them, people who might believe in God in a different way. Or maybe they just enjoy killing, like dictators or mass murderers."

"We could talk about genocide, but that's a topic for another day. Martin, can you give us any other examples where fear causes crime?"

"People commit crimes of passion when they fear losing someone they love."

"Then we agree fear is always there, a cause or effect of every crime, whether it's street crime, gang crime, or some other crime. But what about the fears we carry that have nothing to do with crime?"

His students went silent again, unwilling to admit their fears. Their instructor put a few of his own on the table.

"I fear things I don't know. I fear God. I fear death…"

Professor Ryan asked no more questions, letting the death thought hang as a starting point for next week's class.

"A Greek philosopher said when we teach, we learn. I thank you for everything you helped me learn today. For next week, I want you to think about all the times you caused someone to fear *you*. On the flip side, be ready to talk about all the people and incidents that have ever made *you* afraid, all the times when you really felt scared."

He tapped the quote on the board.

"Aim high, ignore failure, and keep believing in yourselves. Truth is always the right answer. Think hard about fear, confront it and stare it down. Now go have a great week and stay out of trouble."

A guard entered the classroom and wedged the door open.

"Thank you, Dr. Ryan. Single file, men, so we can get you back to your cells."

CONCEALED
IDENTITIES

Cryptic two-word emails appeared in Robert's inbox on three consecutive mornings, "character, misjudged" on Thursday, "consequences, unintended" on Friday, and "forgiveness, withheld" on Saturday. The negative theme made it likely the anonymous sender, "Researcher," was someone he'd wronged.

Snow or its threat had darkened Vermont skies for over a week. Sunday brought back the sun with single-digit midwinter temperatures, the ducts in his rented house pouring heat in a losing battle against the chill. Robert rolled out of bed into midlife crisis. Forty-three years old, a man just past his prime, he'd watched it slip away the night before at the Nickel Dime Tavern. Silent, indifferent women sitting at the bar confirmed his downgraded status, their thumbs busily texting. After two drinks and no conversation with anyone, he'd gone home alone.

Connecting with an available woman had once been routine, innocent greetings leading to the verbal tango of seduction and a mating dance. Now preempted by younger men, he'd become old overnight, facing a not-so-distant mortality.

Robert South, fiction writing professor at Montverde College, had published a dozen short stories and two novels. The first, "Presumed Dead," told the story of a man who narrowly escaped

Nine Eleven and never went home, disappearing to a new life with a fabricated identity. The book drew rave reviews but sold poorly. The second novel, "Sympathetic Jury," portrayed a woman wrongfully acquitted in the murder of her husband. Panned by critics, it became a surprise bestseller. A third half-written novel remained stuck in his computer.

It was too cold to fetch the newspaper. He made a cup of hot cocoa and mulled strategies to unblock his tale of a virtuous state legislator fighting a political machine. The book could be resuscitated by corrupting the protagonist, the temptation of a hero and his tragic fall a story more compelling and easier to write. The option presented Robert the same moral dilemma as his fictional character, stay the course or sell out.

He tidied the kitchen and checked his computer, braced for yet another mysterious email. The unknown party had sent "trust, misplaced," a fourth thought in a growing file of regrets. Robert considered replying with "Who are you?" But such a response risked encouraging the sender and extending the game.

A second email reminded him to attend the annual President's Party Friday night at the mansion, the social event of the year for a college located in the state capital. His attendance mandatory as a faculty celebrity, Robert would mingle with power elites. Annually, the governor, corporate lobbyists, and lawmakers conducted quiet business at this lavish ball in the dead of winter. A continuous line of heated limousines shuttled hundreds of guests from nearby parking lots to the home's circular drive and pillared portico. Smiling hospitality staff greeted invitees, hanging coats on carts color-coded with bright ribbons. In excessive opulence, an army of servers in white jackets circulated trays of food and drinks.

At previous galas, he'd discovered the few unattached women were on assignment, paid representatives advancing agendas for their legislative or corporate bosses. Robert checked his closet for an appropriate suit and tie before sitting down to resume work on his unfinished novel. Sunday was his day to write.

***

The enormous mansion easily accommodated a long guest list, including an intentionally tardy young senator checking his overcoat at the blue cart. The high-ceilinged ground floor featured a cavernous reception area, oversized doorways leading counter-clockwise to a dining hall, kitchen, bar, billiard room-library, and back to the front parlor. The spacious rooms interconnected in a floor plan from a whodunit board game. Palming a scotch, the not yet recognized senator took his first orbit. Loud laughter interrupted quiet conversations as very important people told each other how great they looked.

He spotted a striking woman sitting alone in the library, perhaps the wife of a lobbyist or legislator. Unsmiling, her blonde hair pinned in a tight bun, looking sophisticated and high-maintenance in a black cocktail dress, she held her clutch purse with a detached air of nobility. Ten minutes later, on his second loop, he edged through clusters of people to find her in the same chair, still disengaged. He approached posing as a familiar friend.

"Is someone getting you a drink?" he asked.

"No. I'm here alone."

"May I get you one?"

"You're not wearing a white jacket."

"Tonight, we're all servers. You look overlooked."

"I've already reached my quota, thank you."

"May I introduce myself?"

"Not if you're hoping to take me to bed. We can't know each other's names."

"What gave me away?"

"The hungry look of a man on the hunt."

"And now I'm the prey?"

"It's the law of the jungle," she said.

"Shouldn't you court me first?"

"No. My game, my rules."

"When do we play?"

"Now. I've got ninety minutes. Do you live far from here?"

"Two blocks. I walked."

"Perfect," she said. "We'll take my car."

The heated seats of her luxury sedan warmed quickly on the short ride. She had played this game before. In his bedroom, she disrobed, draping her clothing over a chair. Her ravenous, scented kiss took the chill out of the room.

"Seventy-five minutes left," she whispered. "Better make them count."

"What's my lady's pleasure?" he asked.

"Me on top. You get to watch."

On a warm ocean, they surfed in tandem, paddling and riding wave after wave until one last surge carried them all the way to the beach.

With three minutes remaining, her car's engine started and a button lowered the window.

"I had a very nice time," she said.

"I did, too. Wish we didn't have to break up."

"We never met and we don't know each other. The past ninety minutes never happened."

She backed her car into the street and was gone.

***

Robert sighed as he read the scene just written. Criticism of his second novel had eroded confidence. He'd allowed his hero to taste sinful pleasure, sell his soul and the sworn ethics of public office. The sketch fit the story, but left him imagining a book reviewer's objection: "Straining credibility, the protagonist meets a beautiful stranger and is offered anonymous sex within sixty seconds. South injects the character with his own sexist fantasy."

Writing about the President's Party presented a second problem. The thinly disguised setting jeopardized his employment. The female character prophesized the scene's fate when she insisted the encounter "never happened." Robert agreed, dutifully pressing the backspace key, watching each of the forty-three lines erase as the computer expunged the passage. He'd find another way to compromise the character. The rejected segment had wasted a precious hour of Sunday writing time. As he retrieved the newspaper from the icy driveway, unnamed characters in the deleted passage pointed to a single, troubling truth.

Robert did not know *his* real name.

Born in Montreal to Marie LeBlanc and Timothy South, a custodian at McGill University, he'd watched his father shovel decades of snow from McGill sidewalks, qualifying his son for free tuition. Worn out, Timothy passed away at age sixty-three. Keeping a promise to her deceased husband, Marie took Robert aside at the gravesite.

"Your father wanted you to know the truth. South was not his real name."

"It was an alias?"

"Yes. He came to Canada in 1968 from the United States to escape the draft. He chose the name 'South' because his home was in that direction."

"That means I'm an American."

"Yes, but you can't prove it."

"What *is* our real name?"

"I don't know. He never contacted his family. We never talked about it."

"Assumed names, concealed identities, we've all been living a lie."

"I'm sorry. Your father loved you but he kept his secret safe from everyone."

Three years later, Robert still felt lost. Some writers picked pseudonyms. His had been picked for him. Names were important, to identify parents and children, ancestors and descendants. His expatriated late father had cut down the family tree.

Robert saw the irony, a career devoted to writing invented stories while living one. He'd written his first novel about a man assuming a fake identity long before he'd learned the truth about his own. He guessed some inherited behavioral trait deep in his psyche kept him from committing to a relationship or a permanent home.

Returning to the keyboard, his revised plot probed protagonist weakness. Crushed by the political machine and denied reelection, the defeated hero's downfall also exposed his corrupt antagonists. Robert mined this creative vein from afternoon to sunset, internal and external conflicts giving the story new life.

Satisfied, he bundled up and hiked through the freezing night to find a hot supper.

***

Monday brought biting wind and another email message, "hope, abandoned," an epitaph for dead, unfinished novels. After mushing to work, Robert sat at a long conference table in his office, awaiting a new rotation of candidates for Master of Fine Arts, Creative Fiction. The two-week residency divided class time between academic study and work on a creative fiction thesis, either a novel or a short story collection.

Five students joined Robert at the table, two men and three women. Introducing himself, he asked each to give name, occupation, and writing project. Sam the lawyer, legal mystery; recently-widowed Claire, story collection; Phil, retired engineer, science fiction; Ellen, retired teacher, historical romance; Celeste, financial officer for a New Jersey city, literary novel.

Robert passed out copies of the five application manuscripts so his students could read each other's work. A schedule listed the week's activities.

"Our mornings will be structured, with roundtable discussions and critiques of your writing. Afternoons, evenings, and weekends, you'll be free to attend panels and workshops with visiting writers and agents. Ellen?"

"When will we get one-on-one instruction?"

"On a conference day designated for each of you. Going around the table, today will be Sam, followed by Claire, Phil, and yourself. Friday, I'll meet with Celeste. Make an afternoon appointment that doesn't conflict with any workshop you want to attend. We'll discuss strategies to strengthen your manuscript and plan your independent study, so you can work at your own pace when you return home. If you hit a snag, my office and home phone numbers are listed with my email address. Please don't call on a Sunday."

Claire wanted to know if they'd be taught a writing formula.

"There isn't one. You're all competent. Beyond fundamentals, my job is to help you develop a writing identity, so you can take a unique story idea and find the voice to write it. Today, we'll talk about writing process." Robert hid private reservations about the value of an MFA, in a world where writers earned little or no money.

Monday's session went better than expected with his students volunteering original ideas. These discussions always energized Robert's own writing. But he cautioned himself to be careful with Celeste.

Her information essay and manuscript showed obvious talent, presented by a charismatic, street-smart career woman, single, forty years old, brown hair, sensuous figure, inviting smile. Her writing lit up each page. Descriptions of the rural town and characters in her protagonist's early years flowed like poetry, with colorful dialogue rich in human insight. In class, Celeste missed nothing, a skilled poker player reading everyone at the table, Robert vowed to ignore raging instincts and keep his professional distance.

Tuesday's discussion examined conflict, after Robert's dawn email read "conflict, unresolved." The candidates understood protagonist roadblocks but struggled to define inner conflict caused by weakness, temptation, and guilt. In the afternoon conference, Claire's collection of short story ideas looked promising, as had Sam's outline of legal suspense scenes a day earlier.

Wednesday's email lament, "loyalty, missing," touched a nerve, tweaking Robert's self-doubts about inspiring loyalty or receiving it. In class, his students exchanged constructive critiques in a positive atmosphere. That afternoon, Robert helped Phil plot the story of a future world threatened by a trifecta of contagion, natural cataclysm, and accidental nuclear war.

Thursday's defeated message, "faith, destroyed," clouded a planned discussion of outlining, creating detailed setting, and seeding backstory while maintaining steady pace. Robert's students could not grasp integrating past and present in the same story. A difficult day got worse during Ellen's conference. When he suggested a different sequence for her Civil War romance, she refused to budge from a straight line chronology.

Friday's email, "love, unrequited," made Robert smile, on a day the class would define character and story structure. Celeste believed a writer's soul the key to believable characters. That gave Robert pause. His surname unknown, he didn't know who he was or how his non-identity impacted his characters.

The final hour covered revision, rewriting and self-editing. At its conclusion, the five candidates stood and applauded their instructor, a touching, unexpected moment. Robert said goodbye to four of them, Celeste scheduled to return at three. He remained in his office, reviewing her outline and manuscript. Waiting for their conference, his concerns about self-restraint replayed a bad memory, of a past indiscretion and fall from grace.

***

At a picturesque college in a small Tennessee town, Robert had an affair with the wife of another faculty member. It all blew up when she decided she needed to punish her husband further by confessing. Word of the scandal spread quickly. Robert was summoned to the office of the college attorney, a lean, drawling man in spectacles, bow tie, and crisp seersucker suit.

"Womanizing, seducing a fine woman, humiliating her husband. Mr. South, we're not gonna have that. Everyone loses in a mess like this. Randall and Sally have decided to repair their marriage. We think they'll have a better chance to do that if you go back up north."

"You're firing me?"

"No. You're resigning for a personal emergency, actually the truth in this case. We've already prepared a letter for your signature. In exchange, you'll be paid through the end of the semester, and you get the document I'm holding in my hand. It's a high recommendation praising your work here, signed by your faculty supervisor and department chair. You may list them as references, and they will give positive endorsements in any inquiry from a potential future employer. We're swapping the recommendations for your signed resignation."

"How do I know you'll keep promises not in writing?"

"Yes. An honorable man like yourself *would* worry about the college keeping its word, given your ethical track record. Truth be told, the college needs this sordid little story buried just as badly as you do. We'll honor the agreement, not to protect you, but to shield the good people you have so badly damaged."

Robert signed the resignation and was on his way out of town within twenty-four hours.

***

Celeste sat with a coil ring notebook, pen ready to record. Robert noticed filled pages.

"You write your fiction in notebooks?" he asked.

"Yes. At home, I write notes and scenes at lunch, or when I'm sitting through long meetings. On weekends, I write in notebooks at the beach or in noisy restaurants."

"Working your full-time career, can you finish the book before summer?"

"Writing in my free time, I can finish in four months."

"A bean counter who moonlights as a writer. Such an un-likely combination."

"Both require attention to detail. My work gets crazy in September, when the politicos set budget and tax rates. Ten more years, and my government pension will allow me to write full time."

"Your writing shows great potential, and unique voice. Let's talk about your protagonist. What does she want? How will she get it? Who's in her way?"

"In the first half of the book, the character doesn't know. Vulnerable, afraid to be alone, she trades intimacy for companion-ship. But each new man seeks possession, his seed a territorial claim to exclusivity and control. Her subsequent loss of freedom is suffocating."

"Does she get it back?"

"Each experience leaves her wiser and more selective in a long struggle for self-esteem. She could meet a man who accepts her as an equal, or she might live independently without committing to one partner. I'll know how to write her when I get deeper into the story."

"It works in either scenario. Heighten the conflict, introduce problems in her work as a real estate agent. Your book is character-driven, not an easy story to write. How far along are you?"

"I've written most of the pieces. I'm down to sequencing, fitting parts together in a cohesive narrative. The final editing should go quickly."

"Please send me a rough outline after you assemble the fragments."

The conference continued, Robert playing Socrates, each answer prompting a new question, Celeste receptive to suggested plot points.

"Okay," he said. "When you get back to New Jersey, create a schedule and send me regular submissions in chapter sequence. I'll try to give quick turnarounds with my evaluations and comments. You're off to a great start. Any questions?"

"What is Robert South working on?"

"A new novel plotting the moral descent of a state legislator."

"Let me know if I can help. I'm an expert on how all that government sausage gets made."

"I may call you. Thanks, Celeste. I've had fun working with you."

"I didn't know it was possible to learn so much in a week. Can I buy you dinner?"

"Thanks, but no. I've got plans tonight and I have to hurry home."

Robert saw disappointment in her eyes as he stood and walked her to the door. As they said goodbye, he reminded her to phone if the writing got stuck. Papers gathered, he sat a while, calming his nerves, congratulating himself for resisting strong prurient interest in Celeste.

He trudged home to a cold sandwich and preparation for the President's Party. Find the rubber-soled dress shoes to deal with the ice, put on the overcoat, hike on over there. Robert intended only a short appearance, early escape possible after visual contact with his employers.

Holding court in a small circle of patrons, the president beamed when he announced, "Ladies and gentlemen, I give you Robert South, our acclaimed resident novelist. Hope you're behaving yourself. How's the MFA program going?"

"Great so far, sir, healthy enrollment, long waiting lists. We're seeing talented candidates and emerging writers."

"Excellent. Keep up your great work."

A firm handshake certified obligation met. The program was a cash cow for the college with low capital costs, an untenured, underpaid core faculty, and fat tuition checks. Entering the mansion, Robert had gone directly to see the king, hands free, not yet holding his liquid reward. He hoped the good behavior comment had not been a reference to his exit from Tennessee. It had been years, but such stories had a life of their own in the club of college presidents.

A quick lap would complete his duty. Leaving the bar with his scotch, he bumped hips with a strapless, stunning Celeste. She grabbed hold and spun him around.

"Well! At least I know you didn't fib about having plans for this evening."

"We meet again. Did the college invite you to this extravaganza?"

"My sister's married to a state senator. I'm pretending I'm her."

"Are you staying with them?" Robert wanted the question back as soon as he asked it.

She pounced with a smiling, teasing response. "I have a hotel room. I need my privacy."

"You look sensational, Celeste. Someone should take your picture. Be careful. Male guests here include weak, unrepentant sinners."

"Robert South could be in my photo, famed novelist in seldom-worn suit and tie, barely recognizable without his jeans and flannel shirt. I'm thinking I already know your weakness."

"Then you guessed I'm a man trying to survive in a cold climate. I can't ever seem to get warm. I nearly froze walking over here."

"We should go somewhere toasty for a quiet drink and some writing talk."

"Sweet thought, but we can't socialize as long as you're my student."

"That's too bad. I don't drive home until next Sunday. I was hoping we could have a friendship once the classroom work was finished."

"I'll still be evaluating your submissions, deciding if they meet all requirements."

"Okay then, this summer, after I've earned my diploma, come to my house at the Jersey Shore for a private writers' conference. We can polish each other's novels."

"You're a beautiful girl still in her prime. No man waiting back home?"

"Nope, I got my own place and my own space. I love men, but I could never live with one. I just borrow a man every so often. I was hoping you might loan yourself out."

"Maybe I'll come down to celebrate your graduation. We can talk about it after you complete the program. For now, I have to say goodnight."

Robert put down his half-empty glass, gave Celeste a polite hug, kissed her cheek, and walked away, taking a direct line to his overcoat, the door, and home.

When he got there, he discovered another email from the unknown source.

"We should meet, tomorrow at eleven-thirty, Maple Leaf Diner, two people sitting in a window booth. When I see you, I'll raise my arm so you'll know it's us."

He felt dizzy, symptoms having nothing to do with the combination of scotch, Celeste, and the cold night air. The chance to identify the mystery emailer brought an adrenaline rush. He vowed to stay calm and not show anger.

***

When he passed through the diner entrance and saw the hand go up, he recognized Bobbie immediately, a dark-haired beauty he hadn't seen in nearly twenty years. Robert recalled their last contact while he stomped snow off his boots, removed cap and scarf, and walked the sixty feet to the booth. Close friends and grad students, they'd gone to her apartment, celebrating completion of their coursework. He'd be leaving for another state in the morning. They laughed at the coincidence of names, Robert and Roberta. She challenged his fluency in French, and he played the role of a French suitor pleading for sex, whispering romance language in her ears, hair, neck, cleavage, no translation needed. The game turned serious. They made hurried, half-dressed love on her couch. Afterwards, eyes averted from something that shouldn't ever have happened, he mumbled goodnight and never saw her again.

Bobbie reached over to touch hands. "Hello, Robert. Forgive me for sending those crazy emails. Remember when we kept our writing ideas on slips of paper in cigar boxes? I needed a hook to get you to meet with us. The young lady beside me is Amanda."

A shy-looking girl smiled and stared at him.

"You look great, Bobbie. The years have been kind. You should have just invited me."

"Either way, I'm glad you're here. I've been following your writing career. Your body of work is quite impressive."

"I've had a few breaks. Owe it all to the great writing partner I had back in New York. What brings the two of you to Vermont? Are you here to look at the college?"

"No. Actually, this young lady is celebrating her eighteenth birthday today. Bringing her here to meet you keeps a promise I made to her a few years back."

"Is she a writer like her Mom?"

"No, Robert. Amanda is your daughter."

Shocked but recovering quickly, he smiled and took the hand of his beautiful gift.

At last, Robert South knew who he was.

About the Author

Jeff Boyle's awards for writing attest to his dedication to excellence. The Rutgers Political Science undergrad, who earned his Master's Degree in Administration from Nova University, exhibited the same excellence in his baseball card business, The Baseball Card Exchange, for more than 20 years.

Meanwhile, he also served for a decade on the City Commission in Ormond Beach, Florida. Now this Philadelphia native-turned Floridian is dedicated full time to his writing, and Bold Venture Press is proud to present his first short story collection of literary works, each sharing life's hidden truths.

Jeff Boyle's
SHORT STORY AWARDS

Miss Piano
- Short Story Finalist, 2013 & 2016 Florida Writers Association Royal Palm Awards
- 1st Place Short Story, 2015 Writers-Editors Network International Writing Competition

Concealed Identities
- Short Story Finalist, 2015 Florida Writers Association Royal Palm Awards

Twenty-two
- Top Ten Selection, *2015* Florida Writers Association Anthology #7, Short Fiction, *Revisions: Stories of Starting Over*, chosen by author Marie Bostwick from sixty winning entries
- 1st Honorable Mention, Fiction Category, highest-rated short story, 2016 Writers-Editors International Writing Competition

Guns
- 2013 Florida Writers Association Anthology #5, short fiction, "It's A Crime"

Euro Sky Hop
- Short Story Finalist, 2012 Florida Writers Association Royal Palm Awards

Lindi isn't backing
down from a challenge
this handsome …

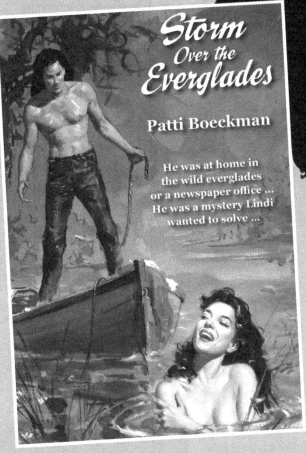

She's left New York to run her family's weekly Florida
newspaper. Now she's investigating a real estate scam
targeting retirees … and she's doing some fact-checking
on the darkly handsome managing editor …

EXPOSED!

Reporter goes deep undercover ...

Clarion reporters Janelle Evan (left) and Bart Tagert collaborate.

(ZPI) WASHINGTON, DC — The *Chronicle's* chief editor knew sparks would fly when he teamed up his two best reporters. Combine Bart Tagert's expertise at probing into political hanky-panky with Janelle Evan's zeal for investigation, and they'll blow the lid off the hottest story in Washington. *But their own story is getting much hotter!*

DATELINE: WASHINGTON
by Patti Boeckman
Available in Paperback and eBook
www.boldventurepress.com

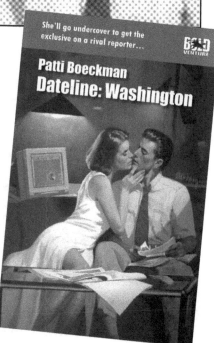

She'll go undercover to get the exclusive on a rival reporter...

BOLD VENTURE

Patti Boeckman
Dateline: Washington